RODEO

a Mary MacIntosh novel

MAUREEN ANNE MEEHAN

RODEO

Copyright © 2024 by Maureen Anne Meehan

ISBN: 979-8-3303-6967-6 (e)

www. maureenmeehanbooks.com

info@maureenmeehan.com

Table of Contents

Author's Note

Go to Wyoming. It is a beautiful state. There are more antelope than people and there is never traffic. You will be greeted with kindness by genuine people.

"Oh, music springs under the galloping hooves,

Out on the plains; Where mile after mile drops behind

With a smile,

And tomorrow seems always to tempt and beguile, --

Out on the plains."

Dedication

Rodeo, a Mary MacIntosh novel, required expert input from some wonderful people who were born and raised in Wyoming and know the ins and outs of the Sheridan WYO Rodeo. I tip my hat to Michelle Meehan, Chris Wyatt, and Mike Cook. Thank you for the photos of the Indian Relay Races and for clarifying the cadence of the race. Despite watching it all of my life, these folks watch it nightly every year and they know what they are talking about.

My family has played a crucial role in my life and I want to express gratitude to my parents, Patrick Michael Meehan and Maurita Redle Meehan. I owe my life to these wonderful people.

My siblings continue to inspire me. Kate Meehan Murphy, Michael Patrick Meehan, and Michelle Lynn Meehan are personal and professional icons in my world.

My four children have shaped me and continue to do so. Chase Palmer Aplin, Allison Riley Aplin, Jonathan Ryan Scarff, and Connor James Scarff are filled with stories of our life's calamities and joys and nothing is better than a home-cooked meal sitting in the backyard dining and laughing about the "remember when?".

Andrea Morrison, my agent and bestie, somehow manages daily miracles and I'm not sure she sleeps. Thank you for believing in our dreams. For the folks who love the escape of a good story, thank you for your dedication and time.

Chapter 1

The Sheridan WYO Rodeo is full of history unique to this quintessential Western town located in the nook of the Bighorn Mountains as part of the Rocky Mountains. In 1926 and 1929, the event took place on the PK Ranch west of Sheridan. It proved people would come to a rodeo. Nearly 20,000 people attended the show and there were 3,000 from 35 states.

The first Sheridan WYO Rodeo was organized by a group of local citizens who wanted to put the small town of Sheridan on the map. The first rodeo was a great success. The $15,000 purse brought professional contestants from all over the United States. A rodeo parade on the darling western downtown Main Street attracted thousands of spectators, and a carnival at the rodeo fairgrounds was in high fashion.

Horses forever changed life on the Great Plains. They tip the balance of power in favor of mounted warriors, and they are prized as wealth. For Native Americans, horses continue to endure as an emblem of tradition and a source of pageantry, pride, and healing.

Indian Relay races have an expansive history that has spanned hundreds of years, and it is considered one of the first sports created and is known as one of the oldest and most extreme sports in the nation. The relay has a rich history and the best of the best travel to compete against each other. This famous race is a way for teams to compete for cash and prizes. Teams consist of a three-man relay two holders and a mugger. The race starts in front of the grandstands with a standing start. The rider tries to take a three-step approach to mount each of the three horses per team. Racers make one lap around the track often changing first-place positions on numerous occasions which engages the crowds in loud roars and cheers. The rider changes horses three times in front of the grandstands using this three-step mount. The holders line the wall which can become dangerously entertaining as often the horses, riders, and holders collide, which causes huge excitement for the spectators. Timers keep track of heats and the teams with the best times advance to the Championship race on Saturday night. These natives are extremely athletic in nature, and they train daily for these competitions. Crow, Cheyenne, Lakota, Sioux, Cheyenne, Shoshone, and other Indian tribes participate for prize money which can be as high as $100,000. The tribes ceremoniously smoke a peace pipe as part of the relay races.

The Sheridan WYO Rodeo is well established as it is highly publicized. E. W. Gollings was an artist commissioned to paint a picture for the first rodeo poster and the entire community of merchants helped support the rodeo committee to ensure the success. Bill Gollings Poster Marketing printed over 10,000 posters and given to folks on vacation to distribute all over the land and beyond.

By 1932 Gladys Accola was selected as the first Sheridan WYO Rodeo queen. This tradition remains a highly sought-after award in that these western cowgirl beauties were judged not only on their attractive appearance but also on their horsemanship skills inside the arena. Barrel racing remains one of the high attractions of the night with cowgirls with extreme skill racing their respective horses

The rodeo was in remission during 1942 and 1943 due to World War II, but it resumed with gusto in 1944 and was rebranded the Bots Sots Stampede to invoke the memory of a series of rodeos in 1914 through 1916 later called the Sheridan Stampede.   Bots Sots is the Crown Indian term for "very good" and the term was used to advertise and promote the Sheridan Stampedes of years prior. While there was still a rodeo, large Indian pageants were replaced by vaudevillian night shows. The rodeo queen program was also reactivated, and the rodeo parade and carnival remained part of the weeklong event.

The Sheridan WYO Rodeo remains a large player on the rodeo circuit and has a very competitive purse, attracting thousands of cowboys and cowgirls of all ages to this day. The town swells in half with pickup trucks pulling horse trailers parked around the fairgrounds for miles.

The Budweiser Clydesdales are transported to town attracting all ages to witness them parade through the town with the glamor and fame that accompanies them. The rodeo parade is attended by nearly all residents of this incredible small town and there are competitions such as the bed races on the hill at the end of Main Street.

Folks build a bed on wheels and decorate the bed to the nines allowing the team to jump aboard the often rickety mobile to gain enormous speed down the hill and onto Main Street.

The parade attracts rodeo queens from all over the West in addition to clowns driving tiny cars and floats with people playing music and throwing candy to the crowds lining Main Street. Native tribes dress in regalia and ride highly decorated horses downtown while waving to fans from all corners of the country.

The carnival includes rides for all ages as well as a haunted house and clowns with magic tricks. This event is held in July every summer and tends to be hot. Families often attend the parade followed by the carnival and then cap off the evening watching the rodeo from the grandstands. It is the "it" event for the summer and people look forward to it every year. It starts on Wednesday and goes through Sunday evening, which is the finale.

There are street dances in the evening on Main Street attracting country musicians and folks often cap off the night at the famous Mint Bar.

The Mint Bar is iconic in Sheridan and has been in existence since 1932. It is nearly impossible to paint a picture of this place with gorgeous old-school woodwork, animal heads taxidermy, and hanging from the walls. These creatures include bison, elk, deer, owls, falcons, rabbits, antelope, and about a 13-foot rattlesnake skin crowning the bar. It is the oldest bar in town and people would be slighted if they had never visited this place.

The Sheridan WYO Rodeo is a must-see for anyone visiting the great state of Wyoming. Most people do not realize that the Suffrage Movement started in Wyoming which is the state where women were first granted the right to vote in the United States.

Wyoming is the home of the glorious Yellowstone National Park which is also the first national park in the land. There are so many wonderful things about Wyoming including the majestic Tetons in the Jackson

Hole area near Yellowstone National Park as well as numerous other mountain chains with peaks over 13,000 feet. The Tetons are the home to Jackson Hole Ski Resort outside of Jackson Hole and are one of the best places to ski in the world.

The Sheridan WYO Rodeo attracts all kinds of people – from cowboys and cowgirls to Native Americans to spectators and "carnies" who run the carnival. It is a conglomeration of people from all walks of life and swells the town once a year with all sorts.

It is the setting of a tragic set of events that occurred in the summer of 2024 and will go down in U.S. history as one of the worst serial killings in the country.

Chapter 2

Up until the summer of 2024, John Wayne Gacy was an American serial killer and sex offender who raped, tortured, and murdered at least 33 young men and boys in Norwood Park Township near Chicago, Illinois, He became known as the Killer Clown due to his public performances as a clown prior to the discovery of his crimes.

Gacy committed all of his known murders inside his ranch-style house. Typically, he would lure a victim to his home and dupe them into donning handcuffs on the pretext of demonstrating a magic trick.   He would then rape and torture his captive before killing his victim either by strangulation or asphyxiation with a garrote. Twenty-six victims were buried in the crawl space of his home, and three were buried elsewhere on his property. Four were tossed into the Des Plaines River.

Gacy had previously been convicted in 1968 of the sodomy of a teenage boy in Waterloo, Iowa, and was sentenced to a ten-year term but he only served 18 months.   He murdered his first victim in 1972 and had murdered two more by the end of 1975.   He murdered at least 30 victims after his divorce from his second wife in 1976. The investigation into the disappearance of Des Plaines teenager Robert Piest led to Gacy's arrest on December 21, 1978.

His conviction for thirty-three murders then covered the most homicides in United States history. Gacy was sentenced to death on March 13, 1980.He was executed by lethal injection at Stateville Correctional Center on May 10, 1994.

He remained the most prolific serial killer in the nation until the summer of 2024 during the Sheridan WY Rodeo. During these horrific five days, at least five teens went missing and ultimately were found dead in the iconic town of Sheridan. It remains the worst crime in the history of the state, but also the worst crime spree committed against youth in the country.

In this scenario, the killer carefully sought out loners at the Sheridan WYO Rodeo carnival and most were youths who were juvenile offenders of some nature. Most youth who get into trouble commit noncriminal acts such as truancy, running away from home, violating curfew, underage use of alcohol, and general ungovernability. The more common juvenile offenses include theft, larceny, alcohol offenses, disturbing the peace, drug offenses, vandalism, assault, robbery, trespass, harassment, fraud, burglary, loitering, possession of stolen property, possession of weapons, and crimes committed on behalf of gangs.

The root of juvenile delinquency is improper surroundings which push adolescents to commit a crime. The causes of committing a crime can be domestic violence, parental indifference, and bad habits. Often potential perpetrators are the victims of violence. The mitigating qualities for these youth tend to be immaturity and vulnerability.

Some of the victims in this scenario were delinquent loners roaming the carnival alone without adult supervision or friends. However, a few were not troublemakers, but they just had a difficult time making friends.

There existed a lack of unanimity and people in Sheridan did not notice when the troublemakers went missing. Most were the product of broken homes and poor, single mothers who didn't have the time, energy or drive to care about what happened to their kids. But some of these teens had very loving and doting parents.

The killer was an expert at picking up on the cues and deliberately sought out victims that fit this mold of walking around at the carnival without a posse of friends.

It would be days before some of these victims were reported missing and by then, it was too late. This gave the killer plenty of opportunity for more victims and this five-day crime spree was a high-speed train in this small town.

Chapter 3

Danny was a beautiful meth baby and born prematurely with underdeveloped lungs and an open fontanelle. He was immediately placed in foster care with a woman who fostered for money, and she left him in a dresser drawer without attention unless he wailed. Even then, she might have been passed out drunk with 13 other kids roaming the house or the streets. It was often another foster girl who came to his rescue and found formula to feed him and diapers to change him.

One foster "sister" was his very favorite as she cared for him and treated him like he was the baby doll that she wanted to play with. He bonded with her, and she cared for him daily from birth until she ran away at age 12. He was only eight years old, and it devastated him physically and emotionally. He stopped growing and he didn't trust anyone. He was like a skittish rescue animal. He flinched if anyone made a sudden move.

Being that no one cared if he lived or died, it was natural that he rarely made it to school unless the truancy officer arrived at the foster front door. When this occurred, he would be forced to school and tested and told that he was several grades behind, and he would be demoted. This did not boost his confidence. Therefore, he didn't return to school and his lack of education, lack of nutrition, and lack of love attributed to his inability to fit in.

Most juvenile delinquents fall into the category that Danny did and he fits the mold of a loner. He was underdeveloped at age 14 with acne, poor hygiene, and no money. He did what he had to survive, including stealing food from the grocery store to slipping into unlocked homes to raid anything available. He grabbed vegetables from Wyoming summer gardens and even sometimes slaughtered a calf from a rancher in the middle of the night just to have something to eat.

He had not lived in the foster care system since he ran away after his "sister" left years prior. He lived off the land squatting at abandoned barns and stealing to survive. He had no life skills. But the kid loved the rodeo. He dreamed of being a cowboy. He dreamed of riding a bronco or roping a calf or simply being part of anything. But the opportunity was not even in the atmosphere. He still had a speech impediment, and he could not read or write. The only job he was worthy of according to others was shoveling hay and cleaning stalls. But it gave him a warm place to sleep in a barn with horses and sometimes a hot home-cooked meal from a nice mother of a rancher. He loved horses. He could relate to the skittish ones. He would sleep in their stalls. He calmed them. They calmed him.

Over time, ranchers learned that this kid was special. Special in the way that he could calm a horse. Ranchers talk. They need good hands, and this kid would outwork anyone for a place to sleep in a barn with a horse and this is unique. Most ranch kids are well-educated people involved in family life with family meals and prayers before meals and church on Sunday.

Danny could not spell church or prayer or school. But Danny could calm any horse, and he loved living in a barn with a restless soul. It calmed him. This also calmed ranch hands. They handled the day-to-day and had to break horses and having a potentially great horse who was uncomfortable and uncontrollable disrupted business. Danny slept with the horses the night before the competition.

There were few ranches that had Danny as their wayward son since he was a lad, and he was fairly well cared for as a result of the wives or the daughters of ranchers. He was fed and could sleep in any barn and most ranchers with a problem horse knew where he was if they asked in town at a coffee clutch.

Rodeo was the exception. The Sheridan WYO Rodeo occupied the population for weeks in the summer, and every summer, in Sheridan. Ranchers were busy socializing with families. This is the party of the season cowboy style, and it was worth life-long attendees to tourists. It was on the Circuit.

This was great for residents and visitors but it was not good for Danny as no one cared if he existed.

He could, however, ride in the horse trailer from the ranch into town with any horse that was able to attend the rodeo. He loved the rodeo. He could stare into the eyes of the horses that he had calmed. He felt calmed by them, and he was sure that these horses spotted him peering through the fence as he did not have the money to buy a ticket to sit in the grandstand.

Worse, he had no money to buy a ticket for a carnival ride. He had never been on one. He roamed the fairgrounds each year with amazement and dreams of a future adventure.

The rodeo was over, but the carnival went on late in the night. He didn't have money to buy a ticket for a ride, but he loved watching. He stood to the side of the haunted house and watched teenage girls emerge giggling and screaming. He snuck into the haunted house during the commotion of the girls. He was never seen alive again.

Chapter 4

Sheridan, Wyoming was founded in 1882 and named for General Philip H. Sheridan, Union cavalry leader during the American Civil War. Not until a series of wars subdued the Cheyenne Sioux, and Crow Indians was the area well settled. The arrival of the railroad in 1892 and the discovery of coal stimulated its growth.

Sheridan is best known for its rich Western heritage, encompassing cowboy culture, historic sites, and outdoor recreation. Buffalo Bill Cody, a famous showman and entertainer purchased a ranch north of Sheridan and he lived in the area for several years. He later spent much of his life in the town that now bears his name, Cody, Wyoming. The serial killer Gary Michael Heidnik is based on Buffalo Bill Cody. Mr. Heidnik kidnapped, raped, and tortured six women starting in 1986, keeping them in prison in the basement of his home.

Queen Elizabeth II visited Sheridan in 1984 and stayed at Canyon Creek ranch with Lord and Lady Porchester. "Porchie" as he was called was the caretaker of her horses and they were very close friends. Porchie was close with the famous Sheridan couple William D. Redle and Ruth R. Redle and Queen Elizabeth II had the privilege of sitting next to Bill Redle at a dinner hosted in her honor.   Ruth Redle was seated next to her husband, Prince Philip, Duke of Edinburgh, and she was entertained by his earnest flirting.

Sheridan is the home of a well-kept polo field, and this was an attraction for Queen Elizabeth II and Porchie. They visited the polo fields during their visit and also went to the Brinton Museum which is a famous museum rich in heritage from the area. This masterpiece connects people to the past, present, and future of the American West through its historic Quarter Circle A ranch. Fine art and American Indian art collections line this historic museum.

Wyoming women were the first in the nation to vote, serve on juries, and hold public office. In 1869, Wyoming's territorial legislature became the first government in the world to grant "female suffrage" by enacting a bill granting women the right to vote.

Curt Gowdy was born in Green River, Wyoming, and raised in Cheyenne, Wyoming and was an avid hunter and fisherman, which extended into his career with the launch of his Emmy-winning show "The American Sportsman." The program featured Gowdy taking celebrities on outdoor adventures and ran on ABC for over 20 years.

King's Saddlery is one of the world's finest tack stores and has a storefront brick and mortar on Main Street in the center of Sheridan. It also has a famous museum in the back containing Western heritage of all dates.

The WYO Theater is an Art Deco masterpiece, and the city's public art projects have turned every corner into a celebration of local culture.

Wyoming's legendary meeting place is the Mint Bar across the street from King's Saddlery in the heart of Sheridan. It is known as a place for cowboys, ranchers, and dudes to tip a cold one, kick back, or more often than not, kick it up a notch. Laying the foundation for countless tall tales, it's no wonder the phrase "Meet you at the Mint" is used all over the world.

Chapter 5

Korinne was the youngest of five children with working-class Polish immigrant Catholic parents. By the time she came around, they were tired of parenting as three of the five kids were rebellious teenagers, wrecking cars doing drugs, and skipping school.

She was unattractive in comparison to her older sister and she felt like an ugly duckling. She was not good at school or sports and found that her niche was in bullying others that she was envious of.

She had a favorite target, and this girl was a year behind her in parochial school but lightyears ahead of her in all aspects of life. This little fourth grader was tall for her age, and excellent at every subject in school, and a very talented prospective athlete. She also was gifted by a wonderful and well-off family who were admired in the community of Sheridan. Her grandfather was a famous attorney. Her grandmother was artistic and beautiful. Her father was a handsome dentist, and her mother was a gorgeous nurse and college professor.

Korinne had a penchant for bullying this little girl, who eventually developed scoliosis and by the fifth grade was forced into the servitude of a body brace spanning from her chin to her hip bones. This development did not curtail the bullying. In fact, it spurned it. As time progressed, this little girl had to have spinal fusion and was imprisoned by a thick body cast by the eighth grade. She was the target of jokes, but only one person was sincerely mean to her. This was Korinne.

Fast forward to high school wherein this ninth grader blossomed after the removal of the body cast and the emergence of a pretty frosh with a very nice athletic figure. This did not sit well with Korinne as now this girl had the attention of the high school boys.

Korinne made it her full-time job to harass and heckle this girl and even enjoyed spreading vicious rumors about her, forcing this embarrassed freshman into hiding in the library at lunch and running to swim team practice after school.

Korinne did not have many friends as a result of her bullying. People were afraid of her, and they avoided her. This caused social isolation. Combine this with parents who had essentially given up on the job of parenting her, this girl was bubbling with anxiety and anger. She still was not a good student or athlete, and she was unattractive.

In the summer of 2025, she worked as a highway construction flag girl and was deeply tanned but still ugly. High school boys did not ask her out. Therefore, she went to the Rodeo and carnival with her only friend who in contrast was a sweet and beautiful girl. No one knew why her friend was struck by Korinne, but they surmised that this girl was afraid of her as well and if she rejected Korinne, she was afraid of retaliation.

Korinne and her only friend got separated somehow during the Wednesday evening Rodeo and carnival and this left Korinne with carnival ride tickets with no one to ride with. She eventually found her way to the haunted house and went inside alone. She was never seen alive again.

Chapter 6

In 1975, Kiwanis member Jim Ross cooked pancakes and sausage for the first-ever Sheridan WYO Rodeo pancake breakfast on the Friday morning of the Rodeo before the annual Rodeo Parade in downtown Sheridan. Forty-three years later, a group of around 10 members of Boy Scouts of America Troop 117 cooked and served pancakes and ham to thousands of hungry rodeo fans the Friday of Rodeo week in 2018. What remains among each of these organizations is a sense of tradition and by the new organization hosting the pancake breakfast, tradition continues into a new generation.

Organizers within the Boy Scouts note that this event builds camaraderie and raises funds for local Boy Scouts troops. Boy Scout campuses usually cost several hundred dollars, and the fundraising efforts by the boys with the pancake breakfast support these camps.

The Sheridan WYO Rodeo Parade is the most marvelous hometown parade in America and directly follows the pancake breakfast.

The parade begins at 10:00 a.m. on Main Street in the heart of this darling Western downtown. Every year an established theme is the centerpiece for participants to build their floats. Creativity abounds and this is a must-see event in Sheridan.

Hundreds stake out their favorite spot on Main Street the night before or the early morning of, and crowds witness the pageantry of the Native Americans in their full regalia on their decorated beautiful horses riding intermixed with floats, clowns, and the infamous Drum and Bugle Corps.

Sheridan's American Legion 7th Cavalry Drum and Bugle Corps is a common sight in the parade, carrying colors, marching down Main Street, and making traditional music. In 1929, T. T. Tynan started the American Legion Sheridan Post #7, Drum and Bugle Corps.

The Wyoming Congressional Delegation supported a bill in Congress to allow the Post #7 Drum and Bugle Corps to wear the 1877 uniform of the 7th Calgary and to carry the pennant the George Armstrong Custer's unit carried into battle. The uniforms are authentic reproductions of those worn by Custer's men, right down to the leather gauntlets, cavalry hats, and neckerchiefs and the group debuted the new uniforms on June 25, 1954, at the 78th Anniversary of Custer's Last Stand.

Following the parade is the First People's Powwow and Dance which is a one-of-a-kind event held on the lawn of the Historic Sheridan Inn during WYO Rodeo Week. Unique in its pageantry and participation, the Pow Wows feature Native American dancers and drum teams in full regalia, performing traditional ceremonial dances. The canvas of color worn by the natives is indescribable and is a must-see experience at least once in a lifetime. Natives of all ages participate with the backdrop of Teepees and covered wagons in front of the historic hotel.

There is a lull between the parade, Powwow, and the Rodeo that evening. Folks enjoy a reprieve from the excitement and the sun as it is normally a warm summer day in July with bluebird skies and puffy white clouds floating by.

Chapter 7

Chester was unusually tall for his age by the seventh grade, and he had buck teeth and a large head. He was a bully because perhaps he thought he had to be. Nevertheless, he excelled at the craft of being a bully.

He also went to parochial school, and he was friends with Korinne so naturally everyone with an ounce of common sense avoided them both.

Unlike Danny and Korinne, Chester's parents actually noticed that he went to the carnival and did not come home. They did not want to cause a fuss because they were well aware that their son was not nice to others, and they also knew that he had a drug problem and was often out for a day or two on a cocaine binge. They did not want the world to know these things as Chester's parents were both teachers at junior high school.

They agreed to keep it under their hats for a few days. It was Friday and people would be attending a pancake breakfast and then the parade before going to the rodeo that evening. They agreed to allow this likely binge until Sunday before reporting it to authorities.

Chapter 8

The Sheridan WYO Rodeo carnival happens in conjunction with the Rodeo at the fairgrounds and runs from Wednesday through Sunday from 5 p.m. to midnight. Rides are fairly traditional for a carnival and have also included the Tilt-A-Whirl, the Zipper, the Spider, etc. for young adults that are tall enough to ride and then kid rides for the little ones such as a very mellow Ferris Wheel, the Carousel, Bumper Cars, and a Roller Coaster that appears as dragons but operates at a low speed.

New crowd favorites include the Pendulum ride, the Pirate Ship, the Rock Star, an Alien Invasion, the Orbiter, the Ring of Fire, the Astro Wheel, the cliffhanger, the Mechanical Bull Ride, and the Haunted House.

"Carnies" run these rides and share shifts that include set up, testing, operations, breakdown, and reloading on the semis en route to the next carnival in the next town.

Carnies are also called "road jocks" and they live on the road throughout the summer and fall, setting up and tearing down rides, or hosting games to bilk people out of their money. They have their own language, and they don't make very much money. On top of this nomadic life, there typically is no work during the cold winter months so a lot of them matriculate to warm places like Florida. They usually don't have strong family ties, but they are closely bonded to one another and they don't seem to mind hard words and low pay.

When carnival people talk about their carnival family, it's because they work all day together and sleep side-by-side at night in makeshift bunkhouses. The stereotype is a dirty, tattooed outcast whose sole purpose is to rig games to cheap people out of their money. But the reality is that most of them enjoy a hybrid work environment empowering work-life integration and flexible opportunities.

In the off-season of winter, most enjoy the golden days when all roads lead to Gibsonton, Florida. The self-defined 15,000-inhabitant town 12 miles south of Tampa is sometimes referred to as "Carny Town" and is fabled as the place where everyone ran away from the circus. Affectionately, it is also referred to as Gibtown, the last "freak show" town in America.

The Carny vocabulary is traditionally part of "carnival can't" which is a secret language in the form of an ever-changing communication at large, designed to be impossible to understand by an outsider. Sometimes this is called Cizarny, and it is not technically a language, but an argot – sort of akin to Pig Latin.

Being that the Sheridan WYO Rodeo was on the world circuit with large purses and staged in one of the most picturesque Western towns in America, the carnival was well attended by all. The hours of operation certainly allowed for the teenage crowd to stay out until or past curfew for this yearly event and parents were fairly trustworthy of their respective children attending late as it was only a few summer nights once a year.

The folks were well aware that the carnies were an unusual breed but they also respected the fact that these hard-working folks were nomadic and were responsible for the set-up, testing, operations, and break-down of complicated machinery. There are very few incidents in history of accidents at carnivals in the United States and it is far riskier to be in a moving vehicle than it is to go on a carnival ride.

There is low tolerance for crime among carnies and many are family people, and they watch over one another like a large family would. They become close friends on the road, and they tolerate very little when it comes to illegal or irresponsible behavior. They work long hours, and they live on low pay, so the reality is that they must depend on one another as a whole.

The exception to this rule is a woman who is a clown in the haunted house at the Sheridan WYO Rodeo in July 2025.

Chapter 9

Tammi was a runaway from Lord knows where and she hitchhiked around long after hitchhiking was a popular mode of transportation. She was disheveled most of the time, but when she had the opportunity to jump in a freshwater creek or lake, she cleaned up well. She had natural long blond hair and honey brown eyes and a nice figure, albeit too thin.

She had to steal food, and it was not beneath her to turn a trick for cash, which was terribly unfortunate as she was now pregnant but she didn't know it.

She grew up on an Indian reservation in Montana and no one ever had reported her as missing. No one cared. One less mouth to feed. She had been on the lamb since age nine and she didn't remember her parents' first names. She didn't care. She knew she had siblings but didn't remember them, other than her older brother who raped her when she was six.

She had never been enrolled in school and could not read nor write, except for small words that she could sound out. She was learning to read, however, because she had stolen someone's cell phone and listened to this person's e-books. She loved listening to the calming voices of a good story, and she liked books with happy endings.

She hitchhiked from Montana south and was now in Northern Wyoming in a small town called Ranchester. The people were friendly, and she was able to get a job helping an older woman who lived alone on a large ranch. She did whatever chores the lady wanted in exchange for a place to sleep on the hay in the barn with the horses and one goat. The horses all had names, and the goat was called Giddy. She loved her. Giddy nuzzled her at night and kept her warm and safe and she felt loved for the first time in her life.

One day the old lady said that she was taking the truck to a neighboring town called Sheridan to attend the opening night of the rodeo and wanted to know if Tammi would like to go with her. She was stunned by the question as no one had ever asked her to do anything fun in her life. Of course, she said yes.

This kind ranch woman had two "Gold Buckle Club" tickets which allowed them to attend a dinner in the building adjacent to the grandstands and listen to some music before venturing to front-row tickets to the opening of the Indian Relay Races. Tammi had no idea that this was something that people did – especially her people – Crow Indians.

She watched in awe as these athletic Natives raced around the track with bareback horses with a paint strip of a color on their flank which matched with the stripe on the Native. There were four riders competing in each round and the winning time advanced. The crowd cheered with excitement for each heat and especially loved the collisions of the horse and holder and they also loved it when a horse broke free and galloped triumphantly alone along the track.

After the rodeo, the old woman returned to the Gold Buckle Club but not before giving Tammi tickets to the carnival so that she could go on rides. Tammi welled up with tears. No one had ever treated her with such generosity and kindness and a genuine desire to watch her just be a little girl.

Tammi loved the Ferris wheel the most. Being up in the air with a view of the town and the people below was thrilling. She did not enjoy the zipper as she was spun around by the carney, and it made her throw up her dinner. Therefore, with a few extra tickets in hand, before she was supposed to meet the old lady at the truck, Tammi ventured alone into the haunted house.

The haunted house was typical in that at first it had a hall of wavy mirrors that distorted one's image. One mirror made Tammi look tall and thin. One made her look short and fat. It was funny to her. She had never really looked at herself before but noticed that she just might be a cute little girl.

As she continued, the haunted house became scarier, and the music was disturbing. There were creatures who jumped out at her and scared her half to death. And then there was the clown. This clown did not look nice. It looked scary with beady eyes and a menacing grin.

The clown grabbed her by the arm and yanked her to its side and before she knew it, she had been handcuffed and gagged and was thrown into the back of an old rickety smelly horse trailer out back.

Tammi did not know what to do. There were three other kids tied up and gagged in the horse trailer and they both looked terrified.

Chapter 10

Kenny was a 15-year-old man-child who was tall and overweight. He was a sophomore in high school and played defensive tackle on the junior varsity football team. He had acquaintances on the team who were not mean to him, but they also did not invite him along to social activities. He wanted to belong, but he was shy and awkward.

He did well in school and teachers liked him as he was always prepared for class and studied hard for his grades – unlike many other jocks in school. He had a nice family and a paper route on his bicycle before school for a little extra jingle in his pocket. He was saving up to buy a hotrod when he turned 16. He wanted to buy an old Mustang and fix it up. He had his eye on one that had been parked on his street for years.

He went to the rodeo with his parents and then he told them that he wanted to go to the carnival, much like he did every year. In the years up through the sixth grade, his parents took him, but now he was old enough to attend on his own. He promised to walk home before curfew, and they agreed.

He loved the scary rides, and one could not keep him off the spider or zipper or tilt-a-whirl. He was always trepidation to go in the haunted house as he did not appreciate surprises, but it was the "it" thing to do at his age, so he garnered the courage to do a quick walk-through.

The funky mirrors were fun but, in his opinion, that is where the fun stopped. He would dash his large self through the rest of the maze and then head home for the night.

When the menacing clown came at him, his stomach flopped. This clown looked mean and aggressive, and he did not like this one bit. The clown grabbed him by the arm and the next thing he knew, he had handcuffs on his wrists and a gag around his mouth. He awoke to a rumbling ride in a horse trailer, and he saw other kids looking equally terrified.

All eyes were watering and Korinne was crying hard. The boys were trying to keep a brave face. It was a rough ride in the back of an otherwise empty horse trailer. It was noisy and it felt like they were on a dirt road. They had no clue what direction they were heading as they could not hear anything but the noise of the rambling trailer.

The trailer came to a slow stop, and they could hear the crunching of footsteps nearing the rear of the horse trailer It was with great trepidation the sound of the keys unlocking the gate.

Chapter 11

The clown was a 42-year-old nomad with a history of being drunk and a long laundry list of abusive boyfriends. She had married twice but was not sure if either was legitimate or if had she kept track of the divorces. They all ended in large fights on the carney trains and the men were most likely no longer alive. She didn't care. She could not remember either of their names.

She hated children. She was born into a no-name family in Eastern Montana, and she was quickly donated to an adoption agency. She was extremely unattractive and unusually heavy for an unwanted child and thus she was abandoned in a Catholic orphanage for years.

Eventually, she was adopted by a couple who adopted ranch hands and she learned quickly the hard way to be a hard worker.

She awakened in the barn before dawn when the roosters decided that it was time to milk the cows, feed the horses, and trek to the creek for water for the feeding bins. At this point, she was six years old and the stick on her shoulders carrying both pails of water was hard to manage, but a whipping from the ranch owner's wife was worse and therefore she managed to balance both pails – one on each end of the large stick It was a half mile to the river so spilling even a drop was not worth the risk of rushing her pace.

She was deathly afraid of her adoptive parents as she was well aware of her place in their lives. They did not love her. She was free to help them. Nothing more and nothing less. She was never invited into the house. She lived in the barn like a newly born foal. She was not to be heard and only meant to be seen if she was seen doing her chores.

As she matured, she continued to grow unkempt and uneducated and angry and mean. This anger built into a rage after men beat her and raped her and used her. She had never been treated with kindness or respect. This lack of compassion was the breaking party of her being human versus animalistic. She was simply a survivor.

And it was always hunting season. The five hunted and captured in her horse trailer were about to learn of the depths of her hostility and rage.

Chapter 12

Due to his sheer size and potential for use of force, she took Kenny out of the trailer first. She had a horsewhip in her left hand, and she used it on him often to get him to honor her gruff commands.

The four other teenagers were terrified for themselves, but they were terrified about what this freak lady was going to do to them. They had no idea where they were and what her motivation was to kidnap them. By this point, her clown getup was nowhere to be seen and she looked like an overweight, frumpy, ugly woman with squinty evil brown eyes and dirty brown short hair.

Korinne and Chester knew Kenny from high school, and they knew that his personality was that of a teddy bear. He played football, but that was the only time that this kid would hit anybody.

Within a few minutes of her whipping Kenny out of the trailer and then closing and locking the trailer door, they could hear him screaming. The screams sounded muffled but real and they were in the nature of someone being physically injured. The screams increased with intensity and then they diminished until they completely stopped.

All four stared blankly at each other and if one could read any of their minds, the thought bubbles would mirror one another. Something terrible happened to Kenny and they assumed that they were next. They were not wrong.

Tammi, the Montana hitchhiker was next in line. The freak napped her next from the trailer and the screams resumed in the same manner and sequence as Kenny's.

Danny, the juvenile delinquent truant kid with the speech impediment was grabbed next, and although his screams were not as voluminous as Kenny's or Tammi's, they were omnipresent.

Chester, the tall bully with buck teeth was next, followed by Korinne, the youngest of five of the Polish immigrants. She was the last one remaining in the trailer and the freak serial killer showed no mercy with Korinne. This haunted house carnival clown was a victim of bullying and domestic violence and instinctually she knew that Korinne was a bully. The clown took her sweet time whipping, sexually assaulting, and beating Korinne causing such extreme blunt force trauma leaving this girl unrecognizable in death.

All five bodies were stuffed into a small crawl space in the basement of this abandoned ranch house out in Lower Prairie Creek to the southeast of Sheridan.

Chester's parents were the first to report him missing, followed by Kenny's parents. These boys weren't known to violate curfew and both sets of parents were frantically worried Thursday morning when they awoke to their respective sons' empty beds.

The local police were notified, and it was immediately reported to all local law enforcement and to Sheridan's County Counsel. An investigation was initiated and there was a press conference to discuss what could have happened as crime was very rare in this part of Wyoming. It was taken rather seriously that two boys who attended the rodeo and then the carnival did not make it safely home on time. These boys were not friends, and they would not have gone out on a bender together. Neither was known to the party, especially Kenny.

There were no clues as to their whereabouts. The last known location was the carnival on Wednesday evening, but upon further questioning of the Carneys who operated the rides, no one could remember either face. It was like they miraculously disappeared without a trace.

Later Thursday when law enforcement came up empty-handed, the Chief of Police called Mary Macintosh, Sheridan's new County Counsel. They spoke at length about the investigation and Mac informed the Chief that she would call for a press conference with the two of them issuing a joint statement and a question-and-answer session on the local network.

The problem was that it was rodeo weekend in Sheridan and there were activities day and night, and no one paid much attention to the Chief or Mac. News did not spread throughout this safe, quaint community and since there were thousands of people from all over flooding this small town, there were no suspects and no clues to share. People carried on with their plans and the Thursday rodeo events were underway with a vengeance.

Chapter 13

Mary MacIntosh was older now and after the torturous incident at the cabin some years prior when she was with her four college roommates, she had taken some time off from the practice of law. Time healed wounds and she was ready to go back to work. However, she didn't want to practice law any more in the traditional sense. She wanted to prosecute crime. She ran unopposed for the office the year prior. The biggest issue in Sheridan is that there simply isn't much serious crime. It is a good problem to have as a County Attorney, but she was a little bored with prosecuting petty theft and drug cases.

 Now suddenly, she is faced with two missing boys. She had full faith and credit with local law enforcement, but the issue was that these boys disappeared without a trace leaving no clues to follow. Her press release was flat, and she knew it, but she had not had one in years, and the people in town were simply too focused on the biggest weekend of the year. It was not because she was a poor public speaker, and it wasn't due to her lack of striking appearance. She was a tall beautiful smart brunette, and she was single. Men of all types tried to date her, but she was elusive and private and a workaholic. She was flattered by the attention, but the dating pool was small in this small town. There were not a lot of single guys to begin with and there was no way she could date other legal professionals based on her position as County Attorney.

She wasn't too concerned about whether she dated a professional man or a cowboy or anything in between. She just had not met the right guy and she was not going to settle. She did want to marry, and she did want to have children, but not with the wrong guy. She had endured a few divorces with her college roommates, and she wanted no part of a custody battle for the offspring of her womb.

Therefore, she poured her passions into her career and to fitness. She was an avid skier, runner, hiker, biker, swimmer, and golfer and she was plenty busy occupying her nights and weekends staying in shape and staying ahead of her workload. Prosecuting petty crime did not require much footwork so she had open opportunities to work out constantly and it showed in her physique.

She had long, toned legs and a lean abdomen and her long, thick auburn hair trailed her in the wind while running. She was a head-turner, but she was a unicorn. Men were intimidated by her. Some women were jealous of her. Luckily, she had plenty of good friends spread across the country and some overseas, and she kept in close touch with the people she loved.

Chapter 14

By evening, the parents of Chester and Kenny had heard nothing from their boys and this was beyond alarming. Their parents were in constant touch with the police and now Mac and by this time both boys' cell phones had a last ping around midnight near the interstate at the turnoff road to Lower Prairie Creek. The pings were at the same time at the same place, so the investigation led the police in that direction.

Mac decided to make a public appearance at the Sheridan WYO Rodeo and planned to speak to the grandstands of attendees to announce what had happened the night before and to warn parents and children to stay together in groups and to attend the carnival with watchful eyes.

The crowds' hushed whispers would be audible and folks of all ages and walks of life were alarmed. This type of thing did not happen in Sheridan and as a tight-knit community, people were visibly shaken.

Parents stuck around the carnival with their teens and curfew was strictly enforced.

The haunted house clown did not show up for work, which happened all the time with Carneys, so it was not reported as suspicious to local law enforcement. Had someone reported this event, it would have led the investigation to this freak, but she and her truck towing a horse trailer were long gone.

The police were able to look at some surveillance footage not only of the fairgrounds but also of local residents and ranchers who had cameras staked out on ranches to keep a watchful eye on livestock. Wolves had been reintroduced to Wyoming a few years ago and calves and lambs were picked off in the nights frequently.

Cameras revealed various cars and trucks in the area the night before but the activity this time of year was heightened due to locals and out-of-towners attending the events of the rodeo, so it was impossible to narrow the scope of the search.

By Friday, Korinne and Danny's parents had reported the missing as well, so there were four known teens from Sheridan missing. Tammi's parents had not seen her in years, and they could have cared less about her whereabouts and therefore she was not among the reports of missing youth.

It would not be weeks before a local rancher's wife reported smelling something putrid near their ranch and upon further investigation into the abandoned ranch house on Lower Prairie Creek. Law enforcement arrived at her ranch and together they made their way toward the wafting stench, only to discover five rotting corpses of Danny, Korinne, Chester, Tammi, and Kenny.

Word traveled swiftly regarding the torturous manner in which they were killed. There was a serial killer on the lamb and folks in Wyoming and beyond were warned to lock their doors and keep their families under close scrutiny.

This story became national news. No one had a clue who was responsible, so everyone was suspicious. It was an unsettling time as Wyoming had two more large rodeos underway, the first of which was Frontier Days in Cheyenne, Wyoming.

Chapter 16

The Cheyenne Frontier Days arena was Wyoming's first airfield. In April 1911, Guy Stoddard attempted to fly a plane that he constructed himself from the arena floor. Local newspapers asked the Cheyenne Frontier Days Committee for permission to use the arena so spectators could watch the event. Unfortunately, Stoddard's flight was not successful. Later that year, Harold Brinker, a renowned local race car driver, flew to his place from Frontier Park and used it as his airfield until 1913.

Bill Pickett was not only famous but infamous on the rodeo circuit. Bulldogging was introduced to the Cheyenne Frontier Days by renowned black cowboy Bill Pickett of the 101 Ranch in 1904. Spectators were amazed at his skill and unfounded daredevil spirit. Unlike most steer wrestlers, early bull doggers grabbed the head of the steer and bit the lip of the animal with their teeth until the animal was alarmed enough to drop to the ground. Other rides imitated Pickett but for some reason or another, decided to grab a steer by the horns in order to drop it and this grew to be the preferable method both for the rider and the steer.

Buffalo Bill Cody brought his Wild West Show to the Cheyenne Frontier Days in year two of the crowd-pleasing event. Bringing daring riders from around the world, his famed troupe of Sioux Indians and a gigantic parade attracted thousands of spectators. This troupe included the original Cheyenne to Deadwood in stagecoach style. Performing at the Cheyenne Frontier Days several times helped set the stage for the next 100 years putting this event on the map worldwide. This level of entertainment awakened the senses of the wild West and became increasingly popular in the country.

Chris Ledoux was a youth attending Cheyenne's Center High School. His God-gifted skill was riding bareback and he entered the rodeo in Cheyenne at the youthful age of 19. He rode many times at the event, and he barely missed becoming the bareback champion of the world only by one point in 1974. His popularity grew and his family was well known to Cheyenne as he sold music out of a booth under the grandstands in between his performances.

After attaining bareback stardom, LeDoux performed at the Cheyenne Frontier Days six times between 1993 and 2003. The LeDoux family remains famous and treasured in Wyoming and beyond as they were wise and branded their own whiskey that to this day is wildly popular.

The first Cheyenne Frontier Days committee asked Captain William Lewis Pitcher to help entertain folks at the rodeo. Captain Pitcher was in command of Fort D. A. Russell and he pledged the 8th Infantry to march in formation and perform a sham battle for the crowds.

The infamous Mr. T is considered one of the meanest and toughest bulls in rodeo history. This notorious bull was a welcome guest for many years at the Cheyenne Frontier Days. He weighed in at the whopping weight of 1,500 pounds and remained unridden after 187 attempts in rodeos around the land. This streak ended when Mary Staneart defeated this bad-to-the-bone bull on his 188th ride on July 30, 1989. The only other cowboys who had success in mounting this ugly beast were Ty Murray and Raymond Wessell.

Thus far the rodeo circuit would appear to be dominated by men, but the reality is that women have always played a role. Sally Rand was a famous performer who entertained thousands of crowds for years. Her act consisted of dancing with large fans made of ostrich feathers and it was quite a show. She entertained at the Cheyenne Frontier Days once in 1935 and her ensemble would set the stage as the official uniform of the Miss Frontier the following year.

The first Miss Frontier was crowned in 1931 when the Cheyenne Frontier Days committee sponsored the first pageant. All six of the girls who entered were sponsored and each judged based on the number of tickets sold by her sponsoring organization. Miss Jean Nimmo Dubois had the honor of the first crown and her sponsor happened to be the Cheyenne Post of the American Legion. In 2021, the legacy of Miss Frontier was celebrated on the anniversary of 90 years. Many past winners shared their experiences as Miss Frontier, and this representation grew to be recalled as the Daddy of 'em All.

From 1901 to 1914, a legendary horse named Steamboat was famous for throwing riders in sensational fashion in rodeos across the land.

Steamboat was a local to Wyoming and a State treasure. He was named after the noise he made after he was accidentally maimed and a bone in his nose was removed when he was a young colt. Many a cowboy attempted fate on this fierce horse and some were lucky enough to ride him but that did not curtail his fame and notoriety and savageness. It is believed that this bucking bronco is the Wyoming State logo seen on license plates, rodeos, clothing, and accessories everywhere.

Chapter 17

Like most rodeos across the land, it is accompanied by a carnival. These dual events are wildly popular with all ages and normally the highlight of the summer. The Cheyenne Frontier Days is no exception and not only does it attract a huge carnival, but it also attracts performances by famous country and country rock bands.

Some incredibly popular performances include Chris Stapleton and Eric Church among others and it is anticipated that perhaps this rodeo can attract the newly Grammy Award-winning Lainey Wilson and Jelly Roll.

The amphitheater complex bolts out across the grandstands and there are non-rodeo attendees that are there only for great music. It is a mini music festival and draws large crowds.

The carnival in conjunction with Cheyenne Frontier Days is second to none and draws large crowds as well. As with the Sheridan WYO Rodeo, it is often the same crew and rides and Carneys as was the case in 2024.

The haunted house clown freak had waited for her fellow Carneys and was ready, willing, and able to rejoin the gang at the Cheyenne Frontier Days. Carneys come and go, but when they reappear they go without much notice as these are transient types and many have few ties.

The clown freak was staking out her next victim on the first night of the rodeo. She again looked for isolated teens who didn't appear to be bouncing around with friends. She noticed this young outcast wandering alone and noted that she was a Native American and she was sporting tattered clothing and looked poor.

Chapter 18

Rita was an outcast and she had never fit in. Her parents worked the rodeo as handlers, and they were completely zoned into their jobs and tuned out to her whereabouts. She was allowed to roam but knew how to meet them at the tent on the fairgrounds at the end of the night. She normally beat them back, but it was not unusual that they beat her to sleep as their work was physical and taxing.

On the first night of the carnival for her, she watched other kids take rides and play games, but she did not have the money to join. Therefore, she was simply a witness although she managed to make the grave mistake of sneaking into the haunted house.

It was obviously easy to sneak in as there were three ways to enter or exit in order to comply with fire codes. Rita loved the haunted house and normally she snuck in every night. Her favorite area was where the ghosts and goblins popped out of nowhere causing the cute boys and girls to scream in fear. Rita feared nothing. She loved watching other teenagers in dismay because these spoiled brats never had a thing to worry about. They knew that there would be food on the table and where they would sleep at night.

Rita did not have these luxuries in life. Her parents were more transient, and jobs were fleeting. They were constantly on the move, and she hated not having any friends.

She was not enrolled in school as a result of her parents' transient lifestyle and she never knew where they would end up sleeping or if there would be sufficient food. The lack of nutrition was visible in this young girl and at age 14, she still had not started menstruating. She was unaware that this was missing in her life.

The clown freak snuck up on her from behind and snatched her by the wrist, handcuffed and gagged her, and threw her in the back of the horse trailer before she knew what was happening.

Chapter 19

Next was a boy by the name of Chance and he was a skinny cowboy in Wrangler jeans and a plaid shirt. As a rancher's son, he worked from sunup to sundown and the only reprieve from this was school.

His family had a beautiful ranch outside of town near a local township called Orchard Valley. They owned cattle and sheep, and his parents were Basque. They had plenty of money and the cattle were well known as some of the best fed in the region and when they went to slaughter, his father fetched a good deal of money for these grass-fed champions.

Chance was proud of their herds as he was equally responsible for them along with his three siblings. They were all expected to contribute to the ranch, and they all did. They participated in the FHA program and often won annual purple ribbons for their hard work.

Chance had, in fact, won a purple ribbon for his Heffer the week prior and strutted his stuff at the rodeo and carnival that evening. He was a cute 15-year-old boy, and he was fit as a fiddle from his physical labor on the ranch.

He had all sorts of girls following him around the carnival, flirting with this darling cowboy. He loved the attention, and he couldn't wait for September 14 to arrive when he turned 16 and could drive legally with a girl in the front seat of the cab of his father's pickup truck.

He went into the haunted house with a posse of kids, and he was having a blast. He was the tail end of the posse and had no idea that a clown was following him. He didn't see her coming. She nearly jerked his shoulder out of the socket when she grabbed him.

He was thrown into the horse trailer, and he locked eyes with Rita. He did not recognize her from high school, so he was unsure of who she was. But he did recognize the terror in her eyes. She was crying and this was the alarm bell that informed Chance that something terrible was heading their way.

He tried to communicate with her, but the muffle was very tight and his mouth was forced open and his tongue was drying out quickly. She didn't even try to make a noise. She just sat there handcuffed, muffled and terrified.

Chapter 20

Melani was 13 and she had been made fun of starting in the fifth grade because she had to wear a body brace as a result of a congenital birth defect of scoliosis. The brace turned out to be ineffective after two years and therefore the summer between sixth and seventh grade she had to have her spine fused and as a result, she had to wear a body case until the fusion was completed.

It is hard enough to be a teenager in middle school but add to this her scoliosis which caused her to be the laughing stock of her class. The teasing was relentless, and she felt ostracized and embarrassed.

Her clothes did not fit around this large and uncomfortable cast. And in the summer, wearing a hot body cast was miserable. Not to mention that she could not get it wet and therefore was unable to swim or shower for that matter. Her mother had to wash her hair in the kitchen sink in the morning before school. She was unable to exercise due to the cast and she kept gaining weight to the point where she outgrew her cast and the doctor had to cut it off and apply a new, larger cast. She was going to have to wear this larger cast for two more months and she was simply miserable.

Her big outing for the summer was to attend the rodeo and carnival with her family. The town swelled with newcomers, and it was exciting to watch new people in town. And the new people did not know her backstory and no one was deliberately mean to her. She was just a local kid at a carnival, and it felt like she was not the center of humiliation for once in her life.

She loved games where there was a chance to beat an animal. There was a ping pong ball toss across a small moat and the goal was to throw a ball into a red solo cup. There were baby chicks swimming in the moat and if someone was successful and made the cup, the reward was a baby chick to take home.

Another favorite was the guppy goldfish. If one was able to pop a balloon on a wall with a dart, the reward was a plastic baggie with three guppies inside.

She always saved the haunted house for the end of the night. She lived within walking distance of the fairground, so she was allowed to stay a little later and walk home at the end of the night.

She handed the carney her ticket to enter and enjoyed being scared half to death with every turn of the haunted house. As she was about to exit, she felt a strong tug on her arm and the next thing she knew, she was bound and gagged and sitting on the floor of a horse trailer along with two other kids.

Chapter 21

Next was Cody. He was a very large boy and a wrestler on the high school team, but he wasn't very good and rarely, if ever, made weight, and so he sat on the bench. He had a problem with profuse sweating, and he always smelled and had a terrible case of acne. He walked with a slouch and obviously lacked an ounce of self-confidence.

He roamed the carnival on his own and could only go on the rides that he fit in as he was six feet five and weighed nearly 300 pounds. Most carnival rides could not support his size, and this left him feeling isolated. It wasn't his fault that he was born with tall parents who were large-boned. They were also large. They did not have a great nutrition plan as a whole and the mother stocked the pantry with useless fattening carbs such as potato chips for snacking and she made things like casseroles with sour cream and bacon bits and noodles.

He could, however, go into the haunted house and it was fun. Lots of shrieks and screams and giggles and it was dark, so no one was staring at his girth.

What he didn't know was that a serial killer used this hangout as a plot to kill a teenager. He had no idea what was coming when the clown popped out and she offered to perform a magic handcuff trick on him. The offer was exciting, and he was naïve, so he accepted. It was his last, worst decision.

Chapter 22

Terra was a poor girl who was infamous in elementary school for peeing her pants in class. Her mother was known as the town floozy boozy, and Terra was embarrassed by this mounting reputation.

She did not do well in school in part because of her bladder problem and also because she hated hearing about her mother's escapades from the night prior.   It's not that she was not a good student, but she had focus issues as a result of these issues. She was a cute girl. She had light thick blond hair, rose-colored cheeks, and nice teeth. Eventually, she would have grown into a beautiful woman. But the clown made sure that didn't happen That day.

Chapter 23

The clown had staked out another abandoned property – this time an old barn on the outskirts of Cheyenne. The freak remained under the radar with these five kids. It was getting late – almost midnight – and their parents would be wondering where they were.

She decided to take them in the order she nabbed them and she started with Rita. This poor Native girl suffered multiple fatal blows to the head before succumbing to her injuries. The other teens could hear her screams, and they were beyond terrified.

Next was Chance and he was a fighter. He was in good shape from working on their ranch and he did not go down without a struggle.

Melani didn't have a chance as she had limited mobility due to her scoliosis and any blow to the body reverberated through her fused spine.

Code was a big boy and strong, but the clown used a knife and it was relatively quick.

Terra was a nervous child, to begin with, and simply a coward in the fetal position and the blows were merciless.

The clown needed to get out of Dodge quickly as she assumed that these parents would be calling the police much quicker than the parents at the Sheridan WYO Rodeo. And she was right. She took to the road and just left the bodies exposed in the open barn.

Chapter 24

The clown was on the road heading directly to Douglas, Wyoming with the intention of repeating her actions at the Wyoming State Fair. Douglas was about a three-hour drive from Cheyenne, and she had time to plan and reflect along the way.

She was born in Eastern Montana in the early 1980s and raised on a ranch by a couple that adopted her from an orphanage. Her mother got pregnant in high school and had her at age 17. The grandparents kicked her mom and her out of the house after the birth and her mother was a poor struggling single mother who resented her child very deeply. This child ruined her hopes and dreams and had she found out early enough about the pregnancy, she would have aborted.

She did not have a good childhood with these adoptive parents and ran away at age 15, hitchhiked her way southwest, and ultimately ended up in remote Wyoming where she could live off grid and steal anything within her grasp for survival.

She was able to work odd jobs and lied about her age and just about everything else on job applications. She would ultimately figure out how to steal from her employers and that was her method of surviving.

She never had a day on this Earth that she felt like she was thriving and happy. Everything was a struggle, and it wore on her.

She started killing animals as an adolescent and by the time she was in her mid-twenties, she had started killing teens. It first began in remote mountain towns in Montana, and then Idaho and ultimately Wyoming. She guessed that by the time she arrived to work the carnival at the Sheridan WYO Rodeo, she had probably killed 11 or 12 kids.

By this point, the number had reached close to 25 on the body count and her thirst was growing. This drive and motivation to watch these kids express their last breath and bubbling as she exited the highway on the outskirts of Douglas.

Her truck was stolen in Montana along with the horse trailer and she managed to steal license plates to divert attention. She lived in the horse trailer, and it was equipped with stolen creature comforts. It was easy to live under the radar and she enjoyed the freedom of her independent life. She had no attachment to anyone or anything and she liked it that way.

Chapter 25

In 1905, Douglas hosted the Wyoming State Fair. The State Board of Agriculture ran the show since 1923, and the Fair was typically in late summer before school started. It has been ongoing since 1905 with the exception of the depression of 1935 and 1936 and the war years of 1943-45. It was canceled also during 1937 due to a polio outbreak. Like most state fairs, it is a celebration of all things Wyoming and showcases the pride in Western heritage, agriculture, industry, youth, entrepreneurs, artists, and more.

One often wonders if state fairs started in the West, but the correct answer is that the oldest state fair in the United States is The Great New York State Fair. This Fair date back to 1832 and is a 12-day festival that includes typical fair favorites such as food, exhibits, entertainment, a petting zoo, thrill rides, equestrian shows, and other community events.

Douglas was platted in 1886 when the Wyoming Central Railway (later the Chicago and North Western Transportation Company) established a railway station. The settlement had been in existence since 1867 when Fort Fetterman was built and was first known as "Tent City" before it was officially named "Douglas".

The Wyoming State Fair consists of a largely agricultural exposition and rodeo, and it started in 1886 as the "First Annual Wyoming Territorial Fair" near Cheyenne. After events hosted in Laramie, Sheridan, and Casper, Douglas ultimately won the nomination in 1905 to host the fair thereafter. The 101st fair opened on August 10, 2013, and hosted country musicians Hunter Hayes and Brantley Gilbert. Dierks Bently headlined the first-ever sold-out concert in the grandstand,

Despite the COVID-19 pandemic in 2020, the fair resisted cancellation. It continues in full force and is wildly popular.

Douglas is centrally located in the state of Wyoming attracting visitors from all over the country. There are a number of campgrounds nearby making it easy for those with horse trailers to park and often rodeo cowboys opted to camp in lieu of a hotel as they didn't earn a lot of money.

On this journey, the carnival clown chose one of the larger campgrounds on the edge of the fray.

She intended to find a dilapidated barn or house to further her crime spree, and she just happened upon one on the west end of town.

She went from there to the fairgrounds to see about work in the carnival as a haunted house clown. It had been working splendidly thus far. She landed the job with ease and was making her plans to continue her scheme.

Chapter 26

Mac had her hands full with an open mass murder investigation and not one clue left behind. No one saw anything unusual and after the Sheridan WYO Rodeo, crowds left the town and this diminished her ability to question witnesses.

And then she got the call from the Chief of Police in Cheyenne regarding a similar crime scene in a barn outside of town during Frontier Days. It was the break that she needed to find evidence and clues. She prayed for DNA to be left behind and tire prints and fingerprints. It didn't take her long to zip home, pack a bag, and jump on the interstate south.

When she arrived downtown at headquarters located near the state capitol building, Chief Jim Burgess met her at the door. He had just ended a lengthy phone conversation with the Sheridan Chief of Police, and they were putting the forensic team in place. One forensic from Sheridan would join the Cheyenne team and they would canvas the barn for evidence.

Mac liked Chief Burgess because he was a get down to business professional and he had a lot more experience with felony crime than the Sheridan Chief. The Cheyenne Chief had previously worked in Denver, and he was wise beyond his years with criminal forensic investigations.

He asked her to jump in his truck and together they would go to the crime scene. He warned Mac that the scene was gruesome and that she should prepare herself. This was much different than Sheridan as those kids had been left for dead for weeks and decompensation can change the visual intensely.

This crime scene was fresh and bloody. These teens had been mutilated posthumously and some body parts had been severed in the process. He didn't think that the killer took body parts as "trophies" as it seemed that their parts were around, just not attached.

When they arrived, the scene had been already taped off and Chief Burgess retrieved his crime scene kit out of the backseat of the truck. This was the size of a travel suitcase and it contained blood identification and collection kits, bullet hole and gun residue test kits, an equipment and storage case, a 3D Leica Geosystem camera, measuring devices, scales, thermometers, trace evidence collection tools, and personal protective equipment. This was the real deal.

He had her gown up and put on gloves and a shield and she wasn't going to be the one doing any collection. This proved his worth already that this man wanted evidence preserved and this was every prosecutor's dream.

They started with meticulous precision. It would take hours of patience, and this was not her jurisdiction, but she felt like she was getting a free education which would eventually allow her to ask even better expert questions during examination and cross-examination.

She was allowed to accompany him to the lab for analysis by the scientists and she was also allowed to go to the morgue while he talked to the pathologist about autopsies for the five individuals.

After two days and watching and learning, she was able to get back on the road to Sheridan armed with considerably more knowledge of crime scene analysis. This would ultimately help her prosecute this sick perpetrator once they were able to find and arrest what they all assumed to be a male serial killer on the loose.

Chapter 27

She got her trailer cleaned out and reorganized before heading to the Wyoming State Fair complex in Douglas. The carnival was set up and the fairgrounds were ready for the rodeo. The grandstands were to host a few country bands each night which were always big names drawing a big crowd.

She approached the carney's corral and talked with the guy in charge of hiring and he was happy to have a clown in the haunted house. Most clowns want to be out in public and the star of the show performing magic tricks and entertaining kids. She just wanted to frighten children and, of course, harm them. But the Carney guy did not know that.

She changed into her clown suit before the carnival opened and took a stake in the bowels of one of the largest haunted houses she had ever worked. The layout of the haunted house was ideal with nooks and crannies galore.

She knew that patience would need to be a virtue, and she needed to wait until it was dark in order for her to work her nabbing magic. As the evening progressed into darkness, her first victim appeared.

This young cowgirl looked like she was spirited and beautiful, but little did the clown know that she was smart, savvy, tough, and fit. This would be a challenging nab for sure. MacKayla was a rancher's daughter and she didn't put up with any lip from anyone, including her friends, boyfriend, or teachers. She would throw the first punch if cornered and she could barrel ride like no other. She was to compete in a few days, and she was expected to place in the top three.

The clown knew that the law was on the lookout for her by now as she listened to the radio while driving and she therefore took extra precautions and dabbed her bandana in chloroform. She snuck up from behind MacKayla and covered her mouth and nose with the bandana and it wasn't long before MacKayla was out like a light.

The challenge of this method is that she would need to drag her lifeless body to her horse trailer sight unseen. This girl was built like a brick outhouse, and it would require strength to get it done swiftly. She peered out the back door and could see a clear path to the truck and when no one was looking, pulled the girl into the trailer and then handcuffed and gagged her. It was easier than she thought.

She decided that she would repeat this with any of the other four if they looked strong and powerful.

Chapter 28

Eddie was a very intelligent young man who could be described as nerdy. He was an excellent student and wanted to eventually go to medical school to become an orthopedic surgeon. In fact, he worked as a scribe taking notes for a local orthopedic surgeon and Dr. Murphy often exclaimed to staff that Eddie was better at his job than most nurses or physician assistants. Dr. Murphy would say these things in front of Eddie, and it made him burst with pride but blush from embarrassment.

Eddie excelled in school, and he was the captain of the swim team. He showed up for practice early every morning before school and would outwork any competitor.

Eddie had plenty of school friends and these were other nerdy kids that he studied with at night. But most of these kids were video gamers spending far too much time holed up in their rooms and isolated from other people. Therefore, Eddie went to the carnival alone. He wasn't terribly interested in the rodeo portion of the fair, but he loved the rides and the games. He was naturally talented at the basketball free throw contest, and he could hit a balloon with any dart.

Toward the end of the evening, he often finished with the haunted house as it was an exhilarating close to a fun night. He entered after submitting his ticket and he was frightened half to death by a zombie that jumped out from behind a wall. This occurred again with a Frankenstein monster but this time the monster was hiding above, and he was not with view.

As he approached the exit he let his guard down but before he had the chance to push the exit door open, he was grabbed in the arm by a weird-looking clown and was cuffed and gagged before he knew it. The clown had a knife and escorted him to the trailer where Eddie found his friend MacKayla asleep, cuffed, and gagged. He was highly concerned about whether she was dead or alive but had no way to check. He knew CPR and could revive her if unconscious, but he was not a miracle worker and couldn't revive her from death.

After the freak clown left, he watched her intently and noted shallow breathing. This was a relief. But not a huge one in that they were both gagged and cuffed locked in a dark horse trailer by an evil clown.

Chapter 29

Buck was a typical high school cowboy, and his lifelong dream was to be a champion bull rider. He had read in the Wyoming history books about Steamboat the bucking bronco and he wished this horse could have given him a chance on a ride. Buck thought he could survive it. No problem.

He also knew the history of the LeDoux family and their skills in riding. There was such a rich history in Wyoming of champion riders and Buck wanted to be among them.

He attended the rodeo not as a spectator but as a contestant and he had done well enough to return the following night for competition. Now he had a little time to himself to join some buddies who were at the carnival.

They rode the fast rides and played some of the games, which were well-known to be rigged, and then they ended the night at the haunted house. This was a large place, and he was separated from his buddies.

He was about to turn left and step over the skeleton that had red eyes and moaned at him when all of a sudden, his nose and mouth were covered with a cloth. That was the last thing he remembered.

Chapter 30

The Wyoming State Fair was a money generator, and it relied on many factors to be profitable. One of these factors was the food concession and food trucks.

Brenda was a hard worker and she had worked at the food and beverage concession stands each year for the last three. She was 17 and could work at 14 and took full advantage of making great tips over a short period of time. She also had a job earlier in the summer as a part-time lifeguard at the city pool.

At the end of her shift, she had just enough time to do a few rides and the haunted house before she needed to go home. Her parents were very strict regarding curfew and if violated, there were serious consequences.

In the haunted house, she suddenly started not feeling well. She felt like she was being watched, but she knew that was irrational as there are ghosts and monsters and clowns there and it is their job to make one feel this way.

Her growing trepidation compelled her to pick up her speed. She needed to get home anyway. But before she hit the exit door, she felt a cloth pressed hard against her mouth. She tried to scream but that just made matters worse and the next thing she knew, she awoke in a horse trailer with Buck, Eddie, and MacKayla.

Chapter 31

Dallas was a handsome cowboy born and raised in the saddle. He knew his way around a stable and a stall and could ride any horse with or without a saddle.

He was a helping hand at the rodeo and volunteered to assist with gate opening and closing for the bucking bull competition. He loved watching cowboys mount this beast of an animal and wondered in awe how their legs were not broken when the bull was still in the pen acting up.

It was exhilarating to be the one to release the beast and watch the rider hold on for dear life.

After he was done with his volunteer duties, he hustled over to the carnival to see if any of his friends were still around, but it was a busy night despite how late it was, and he didn't spot anyone he knew. He only had time for one ride, so he chose the haunted house.

He cracked up at how fake the monsters and mummies were and he thought it was funny when they grabbed at you. However, he had a change of heart when this freakish clown grabbed him and slapped a pair of handcuffs on him.

The next thing he knew, he woke up in the back of a rambling horse trailer. He saw other kids from his school, but everyone was rather somber. MacKayla, who was normally a bad boss when it came to being challenged, looked terrified. It was for a good reason.

Chapter 32

Mac was back in Sheridan, fielding calls from mourning parents and dealing with the Sheridan Press as well as community leaders. There was mounting pressure on her for not advancing one suspect to date. It had been a month since the massacre, and she had nothing. It was potentially career-ending.

She kept in close contact with Chief Russell, but he was in the same boat in Cheyenne. The fancy 3D forensic equipment turned up nothing. There was no DNA that did not belong to the victims, nor was there ingress or egress evidence of a vehicle arriving at the old barn or leaving it.

The killer was a smart criminal. She carried a push broom in her truck and she eliminated tire tracks and footprints before she left the scene. She wore gloves and a hair net covered by a cap and a mask. They knew enough about DNA to know that a criminal does not want to leave a trace.

Mac was smart too. He could usually predict the outcome of a case before the jury deliberated. She was intuitive and insightful when it came to other people. She felt like she needed to hone these skills after missing the mark defending Michael O'Connor in the trial.

Hyper focused on crime scene photos and analysis, she started considering the circumstances. Both crimes happened during the carnival of a rodeo that was well attended, meaning that strangers are not noticed in these small towns. The crimes happen later in the evening meaning that the perpetrator or perpetrators want swift action in the dark of the night. They must have proximity to the carnival and to a scoped-out remote abandoned property. And then the lightbulb went on.

Chapter 33

MacKayla scooted toward Buck and Eddie and tried to communicate with them in any manner possible. The clown took their respective cell phones immediately so there was no way to call for help and they were in the back of a noisy horse trailer so no one would hear their cries for help. But she was a clever one and wiggled as close to buck as possible and turtled in backward to feel what was in his front pockets. In his mind, he thought she was coming on to her in a highly undesirable time and place, but it was when she pushed on his small Swiss Army knife that he figured out what she was doing.

Buck got to his knees, and she backed her bound hands closer slowly but surely, she was able to get her left hand in his Wranglers and together they wiggled and maneuvered access to the knife.

Eddie watched carefully, noting what she was doing, and started formulating a plan. If they could extricate themselves from these handcuffs somehow by picking the lock with the small point of the knife, they could ungag one another and get out somehow.

Eddie decided that if they could first ungag at least one of them by cutting the tight gag off one of their mouths, they could communicate quicker by using nods to address questions or commands. He gestured to MacKayla for the knife and she spun quickly around to get it in his hands. He then nodded to her to bring her face close to his hands and she reluctantly did. She felt like she should be cutting off his gag and he was not nearly as handsome as her or Buck, but quickly decided that this was clearly not the priority. She complied and bent down near his hands while he tried to carefully but swiftly work his way through this thick, black tight band around her head.

It was taking too long and Eddie, MacKayla, and Buck instinctively knew it. They aborted the mission. They could communicate already with nods and gestures so Eddie then started working on her cuffs. Buck vehemently disagreed with Eddie performing the task as Buck could fix anything as a ranch hand and gestured for Eddie to pass the blade. Eddie understood.

Buck worked on MacKayla's lock and through basically the Braille method of touch with Eddie trying to help direct Buck, they finally heard the most glorious sound of a click and MacKayla's hands were free. She grabbed the gag off her mouth and took theirs too and then they whispered how to proceed.

Buck wanted MacKayla to free him first as he was a big strong kid and anyone who wants to be a bull rider can handle physicality. She got to work with Eddie helping her figure it out and soon Buck and MacKayla were free. MacKayla got to work on Eddie's cuffs while Buck took the gags off Brenda and Dallas. Buck figured that they didn't need to even free Brenda or Dallas right now in the event this freak stopped the truck. They could take her on and overpower her.

That was their plan.

Chapter 34

Mac's lightbulb made her realize that it was time for the Wyoming State Fair in Douglas and this was very likely to be the scene of the next crime. She called Chief Burgess, and he agreed with her logic and he called out an APB to all law enforcement in the state. They would take this Fair by storm and surround the fairgrounds.   Mac called her cohort prosecutor in Douglas and asked him to get some public safety announcements in place. The idea was for the crowd to act as normally as possible so as not to tip the perpetrators off. They decided to crowdsource a QR code to all ticket holders explaining what was going on. In the days of social media, they could swiftly alert people to wasting time.   And that is precisely what they did.

In the meantime, Chief Burgess jumped in his squad car as it was faster than the truck and Mac jumped in her car they would be meeting in the middle of the state in hopes of arriving before dark since that seemed to be the pattern of the time of day of the crimes.

Mac was no stranger to speed. She had always had a lead foot and was consistently seconds away from her next speeding ticket. It is easy to speed in Wyoming as the towns are far away from one another in distance and there are very few cars on the road. The biggest concern is hitting a deer or an antelope, as there are far more of those in the state than people.

She had the crime forensics spread on the passenger seat, and she kept glancing at them along the way. These were rage kills. Crimes of passion with hatred. The perpetrator had to be a loner, angry, and have a history of mistreatment. This person had access to the carnival so it could be a carney. The problem was that carneys were transient by nature and record keeping was scarce so the names of the workers could easily be unknown. But someone had to notice something.

She had her paralegal get a conference call with the parents of all the victims. This took a few minutes, but these parents were desperate. Mac conference Chief Burgess, and they dialogue while driving about some concepts that they were exploring.

The parents were relieved that at least they were doing something and that their respective children would not be forgotten. This criminal needed to be brought to justice for any possible healing and closure.

Chapter 35

They could hear the truck slowing and the road getting bumpier. They were now apparently on a dirt road. The sound was different, and the jumble was rough and they were getting bounced all over the place.

Buck immediately had the idea that if they were on a dirt road that was not well maintained they could use their weight and rush each side of the trailer with the hopes of tipping it. There might be injuries as a result, but it was better than death and they were all convinced that she had this in her plan.

They gathered first on the front left of the trailer and ran in unison to the right and they could feel that their weight was causing a tilt. They repeated this but with much more gusto, as now Brenda and Dallas understood the plan. The trailer tilted heavier to the left on the second try and by the third attempt to the right, they felt like they were really onto something.

They did not know this, but she was only 100 yards from the abandoned settlement and the future scene of the crime, so they had no idea of the urgency of their actions. However, they were now a team, and they had a leader or two, and they felt like together they could do this.

On the fourth attempt, they rushed to the top left of the trailer, and they had the luck of the Irish on their side as the criminal had overcorrected slightly with the prior attempt to tip the trailer, and this time, the trailer was not square on its wheels. It started to roll left, and Buck started climbing the left side wall creating force and motion. Eddie, loving physics, understood immediately and followed suit. All joined in and as the trailer continued to wilt sideways, the freak slammed on her brakes, and this was the momentum break that they needed for success.

Quickly MacKayla told them her idea of each of them splitting up near the rear door and depending on which side opened, they would rush her. Dallas reminded them that the handle should be on the right and the right side was up in the air, so opening the back was going to be a challenge.

But then they heard metal scraping and something that almost sounded like hammering – like a jackhammer or chainsaw. The trailer seemed to slide like a sled, and they were propelled in motion.

Then they heard a vehicle speed away on a dirt road.

Chapter 36

Mac received a call from Chief Peldo of Douglas, and he reported that Buck and Dallas had not shown up for their shifts at the rodeo. This was unheard of. Both boys were incredibly responsible and timely. If one is raised on a ranch, one knows to show up on time.

Mac patched in Chief Burgess who was getting very near the exit to Douglas. Chief Burgess told Chief Peldo to get the police helicopter in the air to scope the surrounding area for anything suspicious. All law enforcement from Sheridan, Casper, Gillette, and Cheyenne were to respond to the Wyoming State Fair and were given specific instructions. There were likely teenagers at risk, so attempted to detain them but did not risk the loss of life.

Meanwhile, the teens are trying to figure out how to get out of this trailer that is badly damaged from the accident.

Brenda wet herself and was crying hysterically. MacKayla was trying to calm her while picking the lock to her cuffs. Once successful, she handed the blade to Eddie to free Dallas.

Buck was occupied with figuring out how to escape this truck of steel. They had no clue what was going on outside this trailer and it seemed like with every beating moment, something terrible was coming their way.

Chapter 37

The Hole-in-the-Wall is a remote pass in the Big Horn Mountains of Johnson County, Wyoming. In the late 19th and early 20th centuries, the Hole-in-the-Wall Gang and Butch Cassidy's Wild Bunch gang met at the log cabin, which is now preserved at the Old Trail Town Museum in Cody, Wyoming.

Butch Cassidy (Robert Parker) was born in Beaver, Utah, a southern Utah town, to British parents who were converts to Mormonism, having both converted prior to their immigration to America. Robert Parker was the first of 13 children, born in 1866, and grew up in south-central Utah. He started work as a cowboy and as such, started to engage in horse theft enterprise as soon as he left the family ranch to move to Colorado. During this time, he also worked as a cowhand in Wyoming, Colorado, and Montana.

In 1889, he turned to bank robbery and robbed a bank in Telluride, Colorado, and fled to Robber's Roost in Utah. A year later, being weary of life on the lamb, he bought a ranch near Dubois, Wyoming which turned out to be unsuccessful. He then fell into what was known as the circle of the Bassett sisters, which some blame on them for his demise into crime. But truth be told, he had already been in that neighborhood for a long time. He fell in love with Ann Bassett and the Bassett family enterprise was associated with criminal activity he was arrested for horse thievery and served time in the Territorial Prison in Laramie, Wyoming where he served a few years.

He quickly reverted to crime and joined associates including Elzy Lay, Kid Curry Logan, Ben Kilpatrick, Harry Tracy, News Caver, Laura Mullion, and Flat Nose Curry and named themselves The Wild Bunch. Their specialty was bank robbery and soon after gang formation, they were recruited by Longabaugh and this adjunct included Ann Bassett and Maude David.

They operated widely in the West including also Idaho and Utah. In 1899 they added train robbery to the repertoire, and this would prove to be their demise. They infamously robbed a train near Tipton,

Wyoming in 1900 and then robbed their final train near Wagner, Montana. At this point, the gang split up and Parker (Butch Cassidy) and Longabaugh (Sundance Kid) fled to New York and eventually Argentina. History has also held disputes as to whether they survived in Argentina.

The "hole" is a gap in the Red Wall that legend has it, was used secretly by outlaws to move horses and cattle from the area. The area is primitive in nature, with secrecy and security that cattle rustlers needed to escape the law. Today there exists a three-mile trail that starts on State land and ends on BLM at the Hole in the Wall.

The outlaw gangs slowly left their oasis of a hideout, but the valley remains. It is part of Willow Creek Ranch, an active cattle and horse ranch located about 30 miles southwest of Kaycee, Wyoming.

Douglas is about 115 miles from Kaycee, but the clown dared not be seen on a major road. She would need to drive on backroads covered in gravel and dust. It would take her several hours to get there undetected, but she could ditch the truck in a ravine that would be challenging to discover, and she could hide out for a few days and then make a break for it at night.

Chapter 38

The dispatched helicopter spotted the tipped trailer and reported it to both Chiefs. The investigation team headed to the coordinates provided and it was within the hour that the five relatively physically unharmed teenagers were set free and brought back to Douglas. Anxious parents awaited their arrival and cheers and tears flowed. It was a close call.

All five gave separate statements to law enforcement regarding the circumstances surrounding their kidnapping and a detailed description of the perpetrator. All were utterly shocked to learn that it was a female. Female serial killers are a unique breed, only representing 16.7% of serial killers. Among the most prolific are Dorothea Puente, Jane Toppan, and Aileen Wuornos – she being the first while engage in prostitution along highways in Florida.

However, the most prolific female murderer in the Western world was Elizabeth Bathory who practiced vampirism on girls and young women. She is alleged to have killed more than 600 virgins in order to drink their blood and bathe in it, ostensibly to preserve her youth.

Mac had dealt with two serial killers in the past – one who injected her client, Ana Bontierre, with the H1N5 bird flu virus and then proceeded to do this to hundreds of prostitutes around the world ultimately causing a global pandemic. Also, when she was with her college roommates at her mountain cabin, a serial killer showed up at their door and managed to wiggle his way into an attempt to kill them. It was a close call. She was no stranger to this psychology, but her experiences were with men. Women were a different breed.

At this point, Mac had been an attorney in Wyoming for over 20 years. Her practice started under the wing of Andrew Harrison in Jackson Hole. Harry, as he was called, was smart as a whip and a good mentor. He allowed her to grow while guiding her and teaching her truly how to be a courtroom lawyer. His personality shined and juries loved him.

Mac learned to just be herself in front of the jury and this developed skill allowed her to fight for Butch Anderson in Sheridan, defending the destruction of his ranch. She also was able to sleuth her way through a Munchausen by Proxy case in Sheridan and she was well established with her reputation.

She watched tearfully as the reunification of parent and child unfolded before her eyes. MacKayla's parents couldn't stop hugging her. Eddie's father embraced him as if he was an infant. Buck's father could not stop crying. Brenda's grandmother held her tenderly. Dallas's mother almost fainted when she saw her son. She was a bundle of nerves.

This reunification energized the investigation team, but it also made them feel even more under the wire and they had prevented something in Douglas that was not prevented in Sheridan or Cheyenne, and there was a criminal on the lamb.

Chapter 39

The clown had a name. Sheila Johannsen. She used to have dark hair and dark eyes and was not unattractive in youth, but her experiences of abuse and neglect and life as a runaway had taken its toll. She no longer took care of herself and covered herself in a clown suit, wig, and makeup to cover what truly was beneath – a hateful, angry soul.

In this dark space that occupied her body and mind, she somehow got some thrill out of making others feel pain, fear, and hopelessness.

She had never had a close call with the law as she had never made mistakes before. She had killed teens for two decades, but always one at a time in remote areas such as Wyoming, South Dakota, and North Dakota. She was now understanding that she had grown greedy, and it had caught up with her.

Now that the investigation team knew that they were dealing with a woman who likely was a Carney, they could send investigators to the operations managers at both the Sheridan and Cheyenne carnivals and rule out some suspects. MacKayla gave very specific information and participated in a suspect sketch, and she confirmed that this was close to accurate. The team used this sketch on an updated APD and the kids who weren't drugged could vaguely describe the truck.

Meanwhile, Sheila Johannsen was creeping along the back roads without her headlights, going slow so that she didn't have to use her brakes. She had a vague idea of where the Hole-in-the-Wall was, and she felt like she was getting closer.

Chapter 40

The search helicopter could not fly past dusk so the team had to take a break. They should have just gone to their hotel and taken a victory lap, but they had 10 unsolved murders of teenagers whose lives were lost and some of their families ruined. They had work to do, and Mac and Burgess were not going to stop until this was solved. It was unimaginable that this monster could possibly do this again.

Wyoming is a big, small state. Lots of land. Few people. And people are nice, caring, friendly, and helpful. It was genuine. Mac had grown to love this and held it near and dear to her heart. She was not raised in this environment and had it not been for Harry taking her under his wing during her first job in Jackson Hole, she had no idea what her life and career would have become. Harry changed the trajectory as he created a career pathway for her, and she will never forget his grace.

When he retired and gave her his firm, she rerouted to Sheridan as it was so much more affordable than Jackson Hole. It was a solid decision,

She loved the down-to-earth people in Sheridan, and she felt accepted and loved. However, she also knew that there were families and friends mourning the loss of five teenagers. And this was not lost on her.

It is hard at times to differentiate between the crimes that one prosecutes. It is natural to feel that this crime happened to you or a loved one and this is a double-edged sword. As a prosecutor, you need justice. As a human being one sometimes needs revenge. It's not a moral discussion. It just is.

Mac felt like three of the five sets of parents needed revenge in Sheridan and she felt like all five of the sets of parents in Cheyenne demanded it.

Her jurisdiction was only that of Sheridan, but she also owed Sheriff Burgess one hundred percent of her support and expertise and, therefore, she had eight sets of parents who needed not only justice but retribution.

She understood. It was not her place to judge. Her job was public safety. For Mac, higher powers were in charge of judgment.

She had to balance her personal feelings with her role as a prosecutor and this was a delicate waltz.

Chapter 41

The area surrounding the Hole-the-Wall is unique but yet not.   If one ventures to Utah and its miraculous national parks and state treasures, one will truly understand the unique value of the West. The West is famous for the Rocky Mountains' Majesty, but the sandstone of Utah, Colorado, New Mexico, and Arizona is underrated.

The backdrop canvas of the Hole-in-the-Wall has been painted many times. But nothing truly depicts this beauty in the beholder of the sunset.

Chapter 42

Mac woke from a reoccurring dream that she had recurring but had diminished, but the fact that it was back meant something to her. She instinctively knew that if she could not solve this horror, these families would never resolve. Nor would she.

Mac had a troubled history herself and it was likely inherent that she solved other people's problems instead of her own. It is human. Mourn for others but not for your loss. It is old.

The loss of Harry was absolutely devastating. He was the only father figure she had, and his wife was her only mother. She passed after losing her soulmate and Mac had to try to wrap her head around losing her only people at once.

She was wildly popular. She was beautiful and genuinely nice and would outwork you and would win. But she was horribly lonely. She could not find her pace in life when Harry and his wife died. They essentially adopted her ostensibly as an adult and she had no one.

To the outside, she had it all. She was athletic, thin, lanky, smart, witty, beautiful... but she was alone. By choice. And the choice was extremely easy. No one measured up.

This was not snobbery. This was honesty. She had non-negotiables for a soulmate, and she was not going to settle. She watched some girlfriends in love, but she had watched some who had settled, and it was obvious.

Mac would never, ever settle. Alone is a good company if one loves herself.

Chapter 41

Magic happens when the sun shines over the Big Horn chain of the Rocky Mountains. It is a magic that the soul cannot script, but if one ever takes an opportunity to experience this bliss, one would understand.

It was early dawn and Mac met Burgess in Gillette. It was 90 miles give or take from Sheridan and it would give them time to debrief before arriving at Kaycee.

They had spent the entire night on Facetime going through the case and they both deduced independently that this was likely the hold-up.

It seemed cliché to them both, but they also knew that the area was remote. The helicopter search could resume if the Casper winds died down. But they did not.

Burg, as she now called him, drove while she navigated, and they negotiated every nuance of the case. They were both so sick about the deaths of the kids in their respective jurisdictions.

Families mean everything in Wyoming and the term family is whatever you decide. Wyoming is a "live and let you live" lifestyle. People love the gossip at The Mint Bar, but they also respect privacy when requested. It is the Old West values with good-fashioned values. A cowboy is sought after for good reason. He is smart, hard-working, sweet, loving, and he won't leave you, Period. End of Story. If you are fortunate to find a true cowboy.

Chapter 42

The Hole-in-the-Wall was not a unique hideaway. It was discovered in the 1800's.

Mac and Burg worked their way en route but not without discussions with his prior teams and hers. He had been in Denver in high-end crime solving and she had ties with federal government officials after the Pandemic of 2008 with the H5N1. She reached out to her connections as did he. They figured that a good team working together was much better than two individuals working alone.

In the meantime, Mac had her private investigator meet with the carnival headquarters personnel in Douglas. She would join them later tomorrow after she and Burg did more work with the Feds, and they could schedule a press conference on all developments in the early hours of the morning.

Burg was smart, but he did not flaunt it. He was tall, witty, and funny. Mac was not looking for anything and he didn't fit the mold of the looks that she outwardly thought were handsome, but he was a rugged and smart man who utilized common sense and his past relations with colleagues to leverage help in an investigation which made him attractive to her in a professional way. Maybe that was a start. She was not sure. But one thing she knew – she needed his help and appreciated it on a high level.

They worked late into the night in his hotel room and Motel 6. She fell asleep in the middle of a sentence with her head on her laptop. He carried her to the other queen bed in the room and covered her with a blanket. She did not stir until morning.

The next morning, she smelled coffee and woke with a startle. She was fully dressed and under a blanket. He was not in the room, but a steaming cup of strong black coffee awaited her on the nightstand. She quickly realized that she had fallen asleep but was grateful for the gentlemanly gesture.

However, she was late for the press conference and needed to change her clothes quickly and freshen up. The press and the communities needed to be updated on the case and recent significant developments and they needed to let the communities understand the danger of the woman serial killer on the loose.

Chapter 43

By the time that Mac arrived at the press conference, Burg was finishing up. Instead of taking credit, he quickly pivoted and announced that he was expecting Mac and that she had a prior commitment. He turned the microphone over to her. It was a genuine class act move and very professional. It was not lost on her.

She was able to present how she came to the concept of a carney which led them to Douglas which led them to concern Douglas parents. But she also did not take credit. She gave all the credit to MacKayla, Eddie, Buck, Brenda and Dallas. She explained to all listening that it was their courage and ingenuity that saved their lives, and, in turn, offered the law enforcement team some clues as to the identity of the perpetrator. Due to these five, they now know how the crimes took place and that it was a woman clown in the haunted house that was at fault. That was a huge breakthrough. Mac noted that it might have gone one if it weren't for this genuine creative, smart risk that these kids took.

The Douglas kids did deserve the spotlight. They were heroes. They stopped their demise, and they hopefully provided enough information to isolate this woman. But Mac wished that there was something they heard or saw that could narrow transient women Carneys who dressed like clowns, as this was likely not a small number. Her investigator was working on it.

Mac decided that it was time that she and Burg involved the Wyoming Division of Criminal Investigation. The DCI was established in 1973 which created an agency of state government under the office of the Attorney General. The Director of the DCI has vast duties and powers including assistance to law enforcement in the investigation and detection of crime and enforcing the criminal laws of the state.

When requested by a county or district attorney, the DCI may assist in the preparation and prosecution of criminal cases and thus cut across jurisdictional boundaries of local law enforcement agencies.

Burg wasn't a prosecutor so this only helped augment his team, but he knew that this might usurp Mac's ability to prosecute the case. It was a sacrifice she was willing to make. Ten children were killed in a short period of time and her ego was not the focus. Her goal as a human was to seek justice for the victims and to stop this animal from killing again.

The odds were that this woman had killed in the past and that she had simply escalated the rate of kill. If true, if this woman got out of the state without detection, she would likely go under the radar for a considerable period of time. If DCI was invited from her jurisdiction to assist, then they would be a conduit for all teams to gather criminal information about who this person could be and establish possible patterns of behavior. Any help would be welcome. They were fighting time.

Meanwhile, Burg had dispatched the helicopter search once again. It was daylight and the winds typical in Douglas and surrounding areas had died down and it was now safe for helicopters to fly at a low elevation. The ground search in vehicles and four-wheelers had never stopped. They stayed out on the back roads through the night looking for any sign of human activity or any hideout.

Burg went with the helicopters. He was an avid hunter, and he could spot movement a mile away. The team welcomed him in the air as he was a calm influence and a hawk eye.

They went up at 10 a.m. and flew low. This truck could not have traveled forever on dirt roads in the backcountry of Douglas or Kaycee without running out of gas. If it had been concealed somewhere, a low-air search combined with ground patrols in trucks and four-wheelers would certainly turn up some evidence.

Chapter 44

The helicopter with Burg was flying low overhead of the head ATV four-wheeler crew Stan Lee. Stan was a blue-eyed brown hair short man with broad shoulders and a daring spirit. Speed was his favorite, maneuvering was his specialty, and he knew the Whole in the Wall area like the back of his hand. He grew up in motocross racing and snowmobiling and anything with an engine was his speed. As long as it was fast.

Burg radioed down to Stan and told him that he thought he spotted a rusted old truck stuck in a barrow ditch crashed with no passengers in sight. As Burg used his binoculars to see if there was any visible sign of life, he could see footprints leading toward the Wall. It was too obvious. It was probably a setup. He warned Stan to be careful and approach with caution.

Stan cut the engine and put out on foot to see about the likely abandoned truck. He could see the damage to the hitch from where the trailer had rolled and also damage to the tailgate. He drew his weapon and slowly went to the passenger side of the truck to see if anyone was in the cab. Burg was right. It was abandoned but there was no sign of blood in the cab, so he didn't think she was gravely injured. He then backtracked to the driver's side and again, no sign of anyone, but there were footprints in the sandy soil. Burg instructed him to photograph them first prior to the pursuit for the preservation of evidence. Stan quickly snapped a shot, not wanting to be distracted for his own safety.

He continued the dialogue with Burg as his pilot managed to remain low overhead. Burg radio alerted the rest of the ground team to back up Stan prior to engagement. Red dust flew in the air surrounding each member of the ground crew's arrival. This red rise in rock formation and the middle of otherwise green grassland of ranches stood out. The lines in the sandstone were artwork in and of itself. It was spectacular scenery. The lines represent planar sedimentary laminations viewed side-on creating what historically is understood to be changes in sediment and/or periods of relative lack of sedimentation and different cycles or episodic deposition.

Causation is wind or water flowing across a surface and these are called partings when the rocks break along or parallel to them. Hence, the Hole in the Wall.

Stan signaled to his team to spread out and surround the Hole as they assumed that she was there because it was dark when the accident occurred, and this was difficult terrain in the dark. It was equally difficult in the daylight due to the heat, and wind and dryness of the air. There were also rattlesnakes that loved to nestle on the shelves of sandstone for warmth and safety from birds of prey.

Once the team was assembled surrounding the Hole, Burg gave the go-ahead to enter, armed and dangerous, and with the order that if she didn't immediately surrender, shoot to kill. This was the Wyoming way after all. Cowboy country. You get what you deserve.

Chapter 45

They entered and Stan announced their presence and shouted that she should surrender, or they would shoot her. There was no response. He repeated his command but again, no response. They proceeded and as they got deeper into the Hole, Stan heard Burg shout, "She's below trying to run for it! Exit and surround her on foot." And they did.

She did not stand a chance to run from these young, fit men. She was older and overweight and out of shape. There was no doubt that she was strong, but her strength came from anger and not from a place of retreat.

They tackled her and brought her down hard on her stomach. Stan kneed her in the back while cuffing her and she was taken to a squad car as Burg watched from above. Burg told them to take her to Douglas to be arraigned on kidnapping and attempted murder charges before she was transferred to Sheridan for further arraignment and charges. He called Mac and told her the good news and asked that she meet him at the county jail in Douglas. The relief brought her to tears.

The arraignment was swift in Douglas and the perpetrator was immediately placed in Mac's custody with the assistance of Burg's team for transport to the county jail in Sheridan.

Chapter 46

It was early Monday morning when Mac entered the courthouse with files in her hand. She'd worked all weekend on arraignment pleadings and she would file the charges with the filing clerk of the criminal court the minute the filing window opened. She requested expedited charges be filed due to the ages of the victims and the gravity of the crimes.

She had her ducks in a row, and she was ready to answer for the arraignment. She wore her navy suit, cream silk blouse, and pearls. She would much rather be in hiking clothes at any other given moment, but not this moment. She could not wait to get this killer charged with murder in the first degree on five counts in Sheridan County. This was a bench arraignment meaning no jury and the judge was the daughter of Mac's former boss, Harry. Harry and Bill Redle were colleagues and gin rummy friends. Judge Redle's only living daughter was now the presiding judge and she was every bit as sharp as her father was.

Maurita Redle grew up in Sheridan and was also educated at Creighton University in Omaha, Nebraska, just like her father and her uncles. Judge Redle was a consummate professional and she expected decorum at all times. She respected her highly. Her father was one of Harry's best friends and Mac entrusted a lot of faith for that reason.

Judge William D. Redle was born very poor. He was the eldest of seven of a migrant combination of German and Irish parents who owned a small grocery store in town.

Bill had a paper route that was later revealed to be also a moonshine delivery side business where he collected the empty bottles on his paper route and delivered them to moonshiners in the area. It helped feed his family as the family grocery store in Sheridan did not feed a family of nine.

He put himself through college at Creighton University in Omaha Nebraska as he was raised Catholic. He was able to survive his meager existence by eating only carrots in law school, enabling him to also pay for his two brothers to be educated as well at Creighton. One of his sisters would become a nun. The other is a wife. His brother Dave joined the military and ended up a decorated veteran for his bravery on Omaha Beach in Normandy, France during World War II.

Bill did not believe in anything other than prayer and education so when he was asked to go on a train by G. G. Postlewait of St. Louis to join him on a trip to Eldora, Colorado for a week's vacation, Bill did not know what to do. He'd never been on a date.

Bill was known by reference due to his grades, reputation, and hard work. It also helped that he was growing and achieving in the legal field. He would become a state-treasured attorney who ultimately sat next to Queen Elizabeth II at a dinner party in her honor in Sheridan.

Bill did join G. G. Postlewait on the train and went to Eldora, Colorado to meet G. G.'s daughter, Ruth, who he married and raised a family in Sheridan.

Mac knew of Bill and Ruth Redle through Harry who had been a guest in their home many times. Therefore, appearing before Judge Maurita Redle for an arraignment hearing for one of the worst crimes in Sheridan was a privilege. The hearing did not take long.

Chapter 47

Rosemarie Rodifer was the Public Defender assigned to the case of the People vs. Anna Pilcher a/k/a carnival clown. It took fingerprints and DNA evidence to give this serial killer a name. She had been killed before and lived a nomad life on the lamb from the law. She was wanted in Montana, North Dakota, and Minnesota for various crimes.

Rosemarie Rodifer was known in town as a public pretender, and she had a reputation for being a horrible person and an even worse attorney. Incompetent, insufferable, and intolerable were just a few adjectives that folks bolted out at the Mint Bar downtown.

Mac despised her but had to work with her and therefore she tried to get along with her. They were in court together often and it was imperative to try to settle cases with this incompetent and rude woman. After arraignment, Mac invited Rosemarie to join her downtown for coffee at Java Moon. Rosemarie never said no to a free breakfast.

"What is your defense?" Mac asked Rosemarie who was dressed in a homely frock and sensible worn-out flats.

"TODDI," Rosemarie replied. The Other Dude Did It. The age-old defense to crime.

Mac gaffed out loud. "You can't be serious. "Judge Redle will direct a verdict to capital punishment if you even try that and you know it," Mac retorted.

"She won't. I will appeal it."

"You will appeal it no matter what," Mac snarked. Thank goodness that Java Moon had excellent coffee. It was the only thing that made a meeting with Rosemarie tolerable.

"You have no DNA. You can't tie Anna to these crimes."

"Awe. I see. I have DNA. I have prints. I have witnesses. I have victim impact statements. I have an arsenal. I'll share it with you. It is my duty to do so," Mac stated.

"Bring it," Rosemarie said as she gathered her muffin and her coffee to go, and she waddled out of the coffee shop and headed north on Main Street back to her office a few blocks away.

Mac stayed on. She did not order coffee to go. Java Moon was a darling café with a Western flare and the aroma of baked goods and good espresso. She opened her file, grabbed her notebook and started formulating the order of witnesses and evidence. She would present the strongest evidence first, which was the DNA collected from the crime scenes in Sheridan, Cheyenne, and Douglas. Next, she would call Stan as a witness as he was the eyes in the helicopter that saw everything that went down at the Hole in the Wall. He would put Anna Pilcher at the scene of the arrest.

As Mac was strategizing her case, Stan walked by on his way to grab breakfast before heading back to Douglas. He was surprised to see Mac as he presumed that she would still be in court.

"Howdy, stranger," he said. "I figured you'd be holed up in court for the day with this whopper."

"It was a quick arraignment. The only thing Judge Redle asked was that I think long and hard about death or life in prison without parole."

"What are you thinking? You know that these parents are going to want this to be a capital crime," Stan said.

"I know. And their feelings matter. I think the last serial killer in Wyoming was Charles Starkweather who was known as the 'Dating Game Killer' and that was a long time ago. And I don't think a woman has been put to death in Wyoming, so I need to think this through. Life in prison would be at least 65 years. She's 42.   That should cover it."

"Do you think that Judge Redle was hinting this to you this morning?" Stan asked.

"I do. Despite the gravity of this, I think she was hinting at this and a hopeful plea bargain. This will be a zoo. It is national news. It is not what she wants. She likes law and order. She does not want a circus, and she is a class act. She won't tolerate a flock of reporters in her courtroom. Everyone will be miserable if this does not happen."

"Is the public defender reasonable?" Stan asked while delivering an exaggerated wink.

"You know she isn't. She's a cow."

"You are berating the bovines," he laughed. She giggled. He was right. Cows serve a healthy purpose on Earth.

Chapter 48

Anna Pilcher was told by her public defender not to waive her right to a speedy trial. It would force Mac's hand to prepare the case in short order. This was going to be challenging, to say the least.

Mac had her paralegal, and her investigator get to work sharing the evidence with Rosemarie. That was required under the laws of discovery. However, Mac did not have to share any of the work product of her forensic dental experts that were used by Mac's team to identify the decompensated victims found weeks after the crimes in Sheridan. Mac knew to hire the best of the best who would be widely accepted by a jury in Sheridan. None other than Michelle Meehan, DDS MS, and her sister, Kate Meehan Murphy, DDS MS. Michelle was a well-respected dentist in Sheridan, and Kate was equally well respected in Douglas, Wyoming. The fact that they were the daughters of a retired dentist, Patrick Meehan, and the sisters of the orthodontist, Mike Meehan, made them the ultimate teeth family. These people knew their teeth!

Mac would start with these talented sisters as her first witnesses. Then she would shift to the local forensic team who addressed the crime scene on Lower Prairie Road and after establishing this chain of forensic evidence, she would turn to witnesses.

Her witness list included the forensics followed by some carnival workers who came in contact with Anna Pilcher. Then she would pivot to the families of the victims followed by teachers and friends of these five if they had family, teachers or friends. Tammi would not have this testimony as she was a hitchhiker with no ties to Sheridan. However, Danny, Korinne, Chester, and Kenny would have these witnesses. Mac decided that this type of character evidence would be short. She didn't want to bog down the trial. Pace was important. Juries got bored with repetitive evidence.

Mac would end with the Cheyenne and Douglas forensic leads as this would tie Anna to the scene of the Sheridan crimes. Her plan was then to rest evidence on behalf of the People.

Mac knew that Rosemarie Rodifer would prepare in her customary lazy fashion and that her cross-examination would be weak and without intrigue. Members of the jury would simply be reminded of the strength of the People's case.

When her paralegal reminded her on Friday that the pre-trial conference before Judge Redle was the next Monday morning at 10:30 a.m., Mac knew that she should focus on jury instructions. It was not easy to win any murder trial, but it was daunting to win a five-count indictment. Mac had never had a murder trial before and certainly not one with the tangibles of the tragic deaths of five teenagers in the community, but also the intangibles of community safety and a stain on the most beloved event every summer in Sheridan.

Chapter 49

Mac's cell rang early Saturday morning. She was sitting in bed with a strong cup of coffee and her laptop, working on jury instructions which would be due soon. She answered.

"Working I presume," a strong male voice inquired. Chief of Police Chief Burgess from Cheyenne was on the other line.

"Burg, what else would I be doing?" she said.

"Running, hiking, skiing, golfing. I can think of a number of better things."

"I would love to, Burg, but this trial is coming at me like an out-of-control freight train."

"I heard that the crackpot public defender would not let this psycho waive her right to a speedy trial," Burg said.

"She's the worst attorney I have ever had the displeasure to know," Mac replied.

"She knows that she can't beat you fair and square, so she needs to take the low road. I think she is underestimating you."

"You are aware that I have never prosecuted a murder one, let alone five of them combined. And that means that I've never been forced to decide whether to pursue a capital case or go for life without parole. Big decisions. I've been a prosecutor for only a little over a year," Mac said.

"You have been a lawyer for a long time. You will figure it out, but I understand your nerves. Breathe in and breathe out like any other moment in time. I believe in you as do a lot of others professionally and personally."

Mac was flattered by his kindness.

"What are you doing today," she asked.

"Going pheasant hunting with some friends. I am driving to meet them now on the bird farm that my buddy owns. It sounds unsportsmanlike but it is not. The birds were loaded into gunny sacks early and they spun around a little to lose a sense of direction and then they were set free. They are startled at first but quickly gain their sense of direction and fly away. So, the hunt is challenging and I am with a group that I've hunted with for decades. It will be fun. At the end of the day, we clean the birds and then one of my friend's wives has a great recipe that's been handed down for generations. We will have a delicious dinner together and have a few cold ones."

"That sounds fun. Thanks for checking in and having a safe, successful hunt," Mac said.

Mac set her cell back on the charger and reopened her laptop. She should be in the office working on the jury instructions, but she had hardly been home and she wanted to work from home in bed with her calico cat named Shannon. The poor thing had been left alone a lot and this soft creature adored her, and the feelings were mutual. She'd rescued her from a shelter within weeks of birth. She was the runt and was rejected by her mother and therefore skittish at first. Now, she slept on the pillow next to Mac and purred the minute they locked eyes each morning.

Chapter 50

Mac's County Attorney's office was located in the courthouse off Main Street in downtown Sheridan, so she didn't have much of a commute to walk from her office up a few flights of stairs to enter Judge Maurita Redle's courtroom.

The Sheridan County Courthouse was a historic building. It was constructed in 1904-1905 in two architectural styles Neoclassical Revival and Beaux Arts. It is one of the most imposing and impressive courthouses in Wyoming and certainly the most monumental government buildings in the state.

This historic creation signified the turn of the 20th century with impressive, authoritative character. This era was a boom in the Northern Wyoming territory. It wasn't added to the historic register until November 15, 1982, which is a bit of a mystery as to why it took so long to dedicate such an impressive building to history.

The brick and mortar are in light stone coned with a gold dome that is visible as if it were the White House or a state capitol.

Mac loved that her office was situated here for a number of reasons. The history alone was incredible and the view was significant from the top floor. This new office was a tremendous step up from her shingle downtown. And it reminded her of her office with Harry in downtown Jackson Hole which overlooked the town square of Jackson and had a view of the Silver Dollar Bar and the arch of elk antlers cresting each corner of the quaint Jackson Hole square.

Mac missed her mentor and partner. Harry was a force of nature in law, but he was also her father figure and if it weren't for him, she had no idea what would have become of her on many levels.

At 10:20 a.m. sharp, Mac entered Judge Redle's courtroom and took a seat at counsel's table.

She organized her file and took copious notes of the goals that she had at this pre-trial conference. She knew, however, that the judge would set the agenda for the near future without her input.

Judge Redle took the bench promptly at 10:30 a.m. She called the case of the People vs. Anna Pilcher. Mac answered ready for pre-trial. The village idiot was late for court. This was typical and did not go unnoticed by the judge.

One of the greatest attributes of this judge is that she didn't care if an attorney showed up on time. She just carried on and if the attorney missed something, that was on the attorney. She was not going to repeat herself.

They discussed discovery and timelines and the Constitutional right to a speedy trial.

"How on earth can you be ready for this trial in three weeks?" Judge Redle inquired.

"I am legally obliged to do so, and I will fulfill my duties as an officer of the Court," Mac replied with sincere dignity.

"This is a tremendous undertaking, you understand."

"Yes, Your Honor, I understand. I can handle it."

"Is there any movement on a plea?" Judge Redle asked.

Mac raised her eyebrows and let out an audible sigh. "Your Honor, I don't see that happening. Opposing counsel and her client have proven difficult at every turn. And, in all candidness, I can offer much of a deal. It's only the difference between death or life without parole. There is no wiggle room from my perspective and that of the victims' families.

They deserve some kind of justice and even with that, their loved ones are not coming back. So, I feel like it is a legal quicksand moment. The more I consider movement, the quicker I sink."

"I've never heard it put that way before, but I understand your perspective. My clerk will hand you the due dates for jury instructions and your trial brief. I wish you Godspeed, Mary. Harry would be very proud of his progeny. He was a fine man and my father, and he had many laughs on the golf course and during card games."

"Thank you, Your Honor."

Chapter 51

Mac was back in her office on the first floor by 10:45 a.m. when her paralegal popped in for instructions. Mac handed her a copy of the deadlines for filing and they agreed to their respective roles when the phone rang.   It was the devil's spawn.

"Rosemarie, what can I do for you?" Mac asked.

"You had an ex parte with the Judge and I am going to get this case dismissed as a result," Rosemarie spat.

"I had a hearing with Judge Redle that you failed to attend. The hearing was on the record in the presence of the bailiff, clerk, and court reporter. Not an ex-parte by definition. Your failure to attend is a problem."

Mac was not in the mood to deal with her now, or ever, so boundaries were important.

"I was tied up with a client," Rosemary softened.

"Again, this is a problem for you. Not a problem," Mac snarked. She could not stand this person and Mac liked almost everyone.

Just as soon as Mac hung up, she fielded another call. This one was a conference call between Michelle Meehan, Kate Meehan Murphy and Mac regarding their findings and conclusions regarding the dental records of Danny, Korinne, Chester, Tammi, and Kenny. These forensic dental experts agreed with ninety-nine percent accuracy that these five were the victims found in the crawl space on Lower Prairie Dog.

Mac was not surprised by the news, but it also made her opening statement to the jury very sellable, and it confirmed in her mind that these sisters would go on the witness stand first. They were both exceedingly professional and smart, and they were also both beautiful. People are attracted to attractive people. It is the age-old Hollywood notion and Mac would use all of the tools in her toolbox to win this case on behalf of the victim and their loved ones and also for a grieving close-knit community. Her passion to win bubbled beneath her skin.

Chapter 52

The weeks flew by, and the lurking trial date was nearing. Mac and her team had submitted everything that was due a few days early just to make sure that no deadlines were missed.

Mac's administrative assistant poked his head into her office and announced, "Looks like you have a visitor."

Mac raised her eyebrows. She had anticipated an unannounced and unscheduled greeting from Rosemarie. It was Thursday afternoon around 3 p.m. and they were to answer ready for trial Friday morning at 9:00 a.m.

Mac stood and walked around her desk to greet this unkempt woman.

"Ready for tomorrow morning?" Mac inquired.

"Well, I thought we could talk about it," Rosemarie replied.

The thought bubble forming in Mac's brain was about to burst into an audible response, but she held back. She knew something was brewing when she did not receive a timely filing of a trial brief. Judge Redle would likely not keep a poker face in the morning.

"What would you like to discuss?" Mac asked.

"Any thoughts regarding a plea deal?"

"I have a number of thoughts, but it would have been prudent to discuss this at the pretrial conference that you failed to show," Mac said curtly. I have since worked around the clock to prepare for jury selection on Monday morning.

"About that. My client does not feel like she can get a fair trial in Sheridan."

"It is the jurisdiction in which she committed heinous crimes. She should have considered that a long time ago."

"It will be the grounds for an appeal if we proceed Monday," Rosemarie said in a menacing tone.

"You will appeal this verdict no matter what so that is a baseless and idle threat," Mac said.

"I am not answering ready tomorrow morning."

"That comes as no surprise to me, but it might rattle the cage of an otherwise calm judge," Mac said.

Rosemarie was about to go down the rabbit hole of bias of the judge, a biased jury pool and likely a number of other excuses but Mac held out her right hand toward her opponent's face.

"Should we discuss a plea deal?" Rosemarie pursued.

"I am ready for trial. I will prevail on all counts. I will seek the death penalty as noted, and your client will be the first female to be executed by lethal injection in the State of Wyoming. She deserves it. The same thing will happen with the pending trial in Cheyenne."

"Well, if we reach an agreement, which won't happen," Rosemarie softened her tone with the delivery of this statement.

"I am not close-minded about this, Rosemarie, but please keep in mind that you failed to file a witness list, or an expert list and Judge Redle is a stickler for rules."

"Well, there will be further grounds for ..."

"Rosemarie. Stop with the threats. Failure to prepare on your part does not equate to grounds for an appeal. The only outcome will be for your client to claim that she had incompetent counsel."

Mac allowed that pregnant statement to hover over their conversation. She watched Rosemarie squirm and search for a retort.

"Life with the possibility of parole," Rosemarie said rather flippantly.

"Life without the possibility of parole," Mac replied.

"I will take this offer to my client, but I will not recommend that she take your deal."

Mac took a long, deep breath. There were a number of things she wanted to say, but she knew that it was a waste of her time and talent.

"You do that. Now if you will excuse me. I have work to do," Mac stated with authority.

Chapter 53

"All rise," the bailiff announced as Judge Redle entered the courtroom. "People vs. Anna Pilcher."

Mac answered ready for trial. Rosemarie did not.

"Are we ready?" Judge Redle asked.

"We have reached a plea bargain, Your Honor," Mac stated.

"Proceed."

"The defendant is pleading guilty to all counts with the understanding that she will receive a life sentence without the possibility of parole," Mac said.

"Is this so?" the judge asked Anna Pilcher.

She cleared her throat and nodded her head in affirmation. Rosemarie nudged her client.

"Yes," Anna said meekly.

Judge Redle inquired about her willingness to plead and whether it was uncoerced, etc., and the defendant agreed. The plea included Anna Pilcher's admission to all murders that she had participated in in her lifetime. The list was long. She was required to reveal what she recalled of the location of the murder scenes with the hopes that the victims could be recovered and properly put to rest and that families of these additional victims could begin the mourning process with at least some closure.

Anna was remanded after all details were noted for the record. The courtroom remained silent. All of the family members were present and there was not a set of eyes without tears. She thanked all present for keeping the decorum of the courtroom and she swiftly returned to her chambers.

Mac conducted all interviews outside the courthouse as was customary. The victims' families simply huddled as a group. Mac convinced them not to give an interview or answer questions yet. This was a substantial case in history and Mac wanted these families to preserve a sense of dignity and peace as long as possible. She felt like media opportunities for these people might be part of the future and she wanted them to have time to contemplate and heal before venturing down this unbeaten path.

It was not even noon Monday, and she was exhausted. She returned the files to her office and headed home. She changed out of her navy suit and into her fitness clothing and headed into the Big Horn mountains for some rest and exercise.

Chapter 54

There was a knock on the cabin door. A former client, Butch Anderson, had offered his place in the mountains for a few days. She had readily accepted his kindness.

She had been there for a few days and was starting to feel like herself again when she heard the knock. She reluctantly answered.

"Howdy stranger," Burg said. "Been trying to get ahold of you for days." She opened the door and invited him in.